Whisper the Guns

Whisper the Guns

EDWARD CLINE

 The Atlantean Press

Published by
The Atlantean Press
354 Tramway Drive
Milpitas, California 95035

Printed in the United States of America

Contents

AUTHOR'S NOTE

Since this novel was finished in 1977, events have over-taken some of the material in it, such as the crumbling of the Soviet Union and its empire. Nevertheless, the story is presented as it was originally completed, except for minor but necessary grammatic and stylistic changes. The author has many reasons for refraining from a wholesale "up-dating" of the story, the chief one being that he regards it as timeless a thriller today as it was a decade and a half ago.

E.C.
January 1992

To the heroes of Tiananmen Square

Chapter 1

Arrivals
and
Departures

Just shortly before the landing of the 12:05 A.M. Cathay-Pacific
flight at Kai Tak Airport, a red Volkswagen jerked to a halt
dangerously close to the water near Pier No. 3 on West Bound
Road over two miles west on the other side of Kowloon. It was
a perilous but perfect, practiced stop, its left front and rear
tires both crowding the edge by an inch. Then the passenger
door swung open and a body tumbled out and into the dark,
oily water ten feet below. The door slammed shut with the
splash, the motor raced, and the Volkswagen sped away.

Three hours later an alert crewman on a Hong Kong Harbour Patrol boat spotted a familiar bobbing object several hundred feet out, drifting in the general direction of Stone Cutters
Island, and directed the craft's searchlight on it. Soon the body
was fished out by other crewmen, all bored with this sort of
thing by now. Also bored was the British officer of the craft,
until he extracted and examined the water-soaked identification papers. "Well, well," he remarked with bright seriousness
to his Chinese second-in-command, "another victim of the
royal flush."

The second-in-command crouched down next to him over the body, ignoring the soggy cards the officer held out to him. Instead, he reached over and rolled the wet, tan head into a better light and studied it. Then he glanced over to his superior. "Wager, Commander?"

The Commander peered at the face grinning at him from beneath the duck-billed cap. There was confidence in the dark eyes. Confidence in what? "Not this time around, Weng. I always lose with you. I'm practically supporting your family now with all your winnings."

"I lost once," protested the second-in-command.

"Once out of a dozen," smiled the Commander, shaking his head. "And that was because we switched. No, Weng, you're privy to these floaters. You must be. Still," he mused, studying the cards again, "you *might* be wrong this time."

"No, Commander," chuckled the second-in-command, "I say this man's murder *will* be solved."

"Well," replied the Commander, standing up, "we can't both wager on the same outcome."

The second-in-command stood up and reached into his pocket, producing a large, gleaming coin, a silver dollar-sized Churchill commemorative. "Flip for sides, Commander?"

The Commander looked down at the dead man and smiled to himself. This one had to be a cinch. This one was too notorious in a notorious racket. There were scores of well-paid informants in that organization. The chief inspector should be drummed out of the force if he couldn't ring this one. He looked up to the second-in-command. "The Lady says they'll solve it," he said.

"Fair enough," replied Weng, flipping the coin. He caught it in mid-air and slapped it to his bare wrist, then uncovered it. They both gazed at the Queen's profile. "Ah, luck is with you, Commander," laughed Weng. "Fifty dollars, as usual?"

The Commander signalled to the watching pilot to head for

port. "Done," he replied to Weng. "Though I wonder why you're in such a hurry to lose so much."

The second-in-command shouted above the roaring engines, "I could have won the toss, Commander!"

來來去去

Chapter 2

Bear
Markets

"We most certainly *do* have suites, sir! Those reservations were made two months ago! One for myself and one for Mr. Sander here!"

"I'm sorry, sir, but our records contain no such reservations," replied the clerk stoically.

"My good man, I'm a frequent visitor to Hong Kong and am as keenly aware of the hotel crunch as you. We have important *business* here and we'd have hardly flown all the way from London and trusted our accommodations to a sweepstakes! Let me speak to your manager!"

The desk clerk blinked once, his only concession to the glowering pair of British businessmen at the counter. He was a tall, muscular Chinese youth, no easy mark for any guest's bravado in the matter of room reservations. Complementing his unusual stature was the ingrained patience of certainty; these attributes made him a valuable asset to the check-in desk. "Your names again, sir?" he asked, fingers poised over the keyboard of the tiny CRT just below the counter. "I'll query our records once again." His smooth, trained voice, capable of making the same statement in French, Japanese, German and

Mandarin Chinese, seemed to offer more than one ray of hope.

"Menzies," replied the first businessman. "David Menzies. And Mr. Reynold Sander. Of Birmingham Micro-Bearings!"

"Sir?"

"Must I explain? We did not book through any service like bloody tourists! We queried you on company telex, and you confirmed likewise the very same day! August 14th!"

"I see," said the clerk. "Private booking." His agile fingers flicked across the plastic letters, pressed a button, and the gray screen rippled out its verdict. The clerk sighed. "I'm sorry, Mr. Menzies, but we still show no reservations. I'll ask my manager to the desk. Please excuse me." With a nod to the tall American who leaned unconcernedly on the counter near them, he turned and strode down the length of the lobby desk and disappeared through an unmarked door.

Mr. Sander, the taller of the two, worriedly addressed his partner, "Oh, dear, do you think we'll have problems?"

"Nonsense," dismissed Mr. Menzies with a wave of his hand. "I've stayed here half a dozen times. That *is* in the records! If they've botched things up they'll have to find something for us elsewhere."

Mr. Sander swung his briefcase onto the counter and took out the orange *South China Morning Post.* "While we're waiting I *must* see if our ad was carried today," he said, eagerly unfolding and snapping it open. "It runs for a week starting today, doesn't it? Or is it next week? What did the agency say—it's part of a group in the financial section . . ."

"Good grief! Let me see that!" exclaimed Mr. Menzies, almost snatching the paper from his companion's fingers. "Another floater . . ." Mr. Menzies' eyes bore into an article on the front page.

"Another what?"

"Another floater! Someone's been dumping bodies into the harbour," said Mr. Menzies, reading and speaking at the same time. "Off and on for quite a while now. This is the seven-teenth. The last time I was here the tally stood at fourteen. Isn't it fascinating?"

"Oh, my, yes," replied Mr. Sander, almost rolling his eyes. "So fascinating. My first trip to Hong Kong offers me the prospect of being excitingly murdered and given a free bath in the bay. All because of a hotel reservation mix-up. Who was it?" he grinned ironically. "The chairman of the Industries Board?"

Mr. Menzies chuckled. "Not our luck, Reynold. No, it was a chap named Kwong Lai. Funds officer for the Federation of Trade Unions here. Someone put a bullet into his heart, then shoved him into the brine near some sampan anchorage over in Kowloon last night."

"*Violent* unions here, too?"

"No, not the kind we're familiar with, Reynold. People *work* here. The powers-that-want-to-be can't get them off the ground because nobody's really interested in joining them. Take this fellow. Just last month, it says here, he'd been cleared of ordering the murders of three Kowloon taxi drivers who wouldn't pay Federation dues or even think of paying. The only man who could help convict Lai was his own body-guard, who'd been arrested on some other charge, but at the last min-ute he chose to perjure himself and withdrew his testimony. Topping that, a court in Singapore suddenly wanted the body-guard extradited to face an extortion charge there. There was nothing for it; Lai was cleared."

"What a confused state of affairs," remarked Mr. Sander. He chuckled. "He wasn't clear enough in *someone's* court, it would seem."

"The police suspect a vigilance committee for having Mr. Lai killed . . ." read Mr. Menzies. "My God!" he exclaimed again.

"What now?" smiled Mr. Sander. "This *is* a facet of you I

never suspected existed, David. David Menzies, chairman of Birmingham Micro-Bearings, a sensationalist news addict? Perhaps he keeps a scrapbook of his horoscopes from the *Telegraph*? Or has a crush on a certain television newslady, known for her interesting necklines on the BBC?"

"Number sixteen was Chan Ha Tze," said Mr. Menzies wondrously, more to himself than to his friend. "Shot in the back, dumped into the harbour . . . early this month . . ."

Mr. Sander sniffed. "I must say that whoever is behind all this has little imagination. Was he Mr. Lai's *old* bodyguard?"

"No, no, man," snapped Menzies impatiently. "Don't you recall the memo I sent you in August just after I returned, on the line of credit I'd established for the company at Felicity Bank? The man I spoke with was *this* man, their chief accounts officer! I had lunch with him! Apparently he'd been promoted treasurer since then."

"Oh, dear," murmured Mr. Sander. "I *do* recall. This *is* disagreeable." He took the paper and glanced at the article. "You're sure it's the same one?"

"I'm certain of it."

"Do you think we ought to inquire about him? I mean, would it be in good taste?"

Menzies grumbled. "Good taste or not, I'm going to ask. The last thing I need is to start involving our business with a bank that allows its personnel to be sacked like so much excess fish!"

Mr. Sander looked up from the paper. "It *does* look bad, now that you mention it . . ." He stopped abruptly and casually folded the paper again. Mr. Menzies, catching some message in his friend's expression, turned to face the American, who had been listening with mild curiosity.

"You have the advantage of us, sir," he stated succinctly. Not only did he not like eavesdroppers, but he disliked men who dressed so casually so early in the morning, in public, without even the courtesy of a neck-tie. He deplored the dress habits of young people.

"Mr. Menzies?" inquired the British manager from behind the counter. Menzies glared briefly at the American, then quickly joined in verbal battle with the manager.

The Chinese clerk came up beside the manager and smiled at the American. "May I help you, sir?"

"I'm Merritt Fury," said the American. "Room ten-twelve. I checked in at twelve-thirty this morning."

"Yes?"

"You are Mr. Chou?"

"At your service."

"I'm to pick up an urgent telegram from you."

The clerk's expression went blank. "Sir?"

The American frowned. "I was told on the phone about fifteen minutes ago to come down for an urgent telegram which you weren't able to deliver personally because of some temporary staff shortage."

"Oh," smiled the clerk. He nodded, indicating another desk across the crowded lobby. "You should see the concierge, right over there, sir."

The American shut eyes that obviously had been tightly shut in sleep not too long ago. "I was told particularly to see *you*, Mr. Chou. At the check-in desk."

"I have no telegram for you, sir. Who told you this?"

"One of the young ladies on the switchboard."

"I will ask, Mr. Fury. Please excuse me." The clerk disappeared again. When he returned a minute later, it was with a frown of his own. "I'm sorry, sir, but no one on our switchboard placed such a call. You had one call from outside of the hotel, but we have no telegram for you. And even if we did, we would have called to tell you to expect a member of our staff with it. We'd never have so inconvenienced a guest even if we were short-staffed, which we are not. I'm very sorry." He turned and interrupted the manager, who had arranged to have Mr. Menzies and Mr. Sander and their luggage sent to another hotel, and explained the problem.

"How very odd," mused the manager. "What room did you say, Mr. Fury?"

"Ten-twelve."

"The caller gave no name or any other information?"

"Only that it was an urgent telegram from George Winch."

The manager scratched his head with a pencil.

Fury smiled tiredly. "I know what you should be thinking: how would the hotel know whom it was from? That struck me as strange, too, just now. Well, I'm not completely awake yet."

The manager put on a silly, apologetic grin. "I'm deeply sorry, Mr. Fury, but I'm afraid all I can say is that we've been the victims of a somewhat curious prank."

"Yes," said Fury. "Very curious. George Winch is in a maximum security island prison in Argentina. If he isn't dead. Either way, he's in no position to be sending anyone telegrams."

"How gruesome," remarked the manager, fascinated by Mr. Fury's words, and unprofessionally oblivious to the stares of Menzies and Sander, who were waiting for him to finish his task. It had dawned on the manager suddenly that this Mr. Merritt Fury, who looked to be about thirty, might be some kind of American law enforcement officer. He had sharp features, close-clipped but slightly wavy black hair, and a thin nose which made the manager think of cutting diamonds. He was definitely what women would regard as handsome: not "pretty" handsome, or "rugged" handsome, but "character" handsome; it was something which started in the green eyes and flowed haltingly through the face. The manager had noticed several passing women give the man long, lingering appraisals, and one, a striking Eurasian, seated with a magazine on one of the lounges in the center of the lobby, he noticed out of the corner of his eye glanced at him constantly. "How gruesome. Did you put him there?"

The American shook his head. "No, that was his own accomplishment." He glanced at his watch. "Well, if I hurry, I might catch my wake-up call. Gentlemen," he said, nodding to Menzies and Sander courteously, then turned and strode away.

When he returned to his suite, Merritt Fury found a breakfast cart and the *Morning Post* waiting. He stood over the cart, momentarily at a loss to remember whether or not he had actually asked for this service when he checked in a little over nine hours ago. He gave up the effort and poured himself a black coffee to brace himself out of the lingering sleepiness, then had his usual cream and sugar in a second cup with his juice and toast. As he munched idly on the toast, he read the *Post* article on Kwong Lai, sped through the lead story from Manila, where, in response to the assassination of a deputy finance minister and the kidnapping of an opposition newspaper editor, the government had imposed martial law, and spied Mr. Menzies' Micro-Bearings ad as he leafed through the financial section. He glanced at the commodities quotations once and closed the paper: yesterday's prices.

He turned once more to the front page. The name of Kwong Lai meant nothing to him, and neither did that of Chan Ha Tze, but Felicity Bank kept tickling his memory for no reason he could think of. He dredged his memory for a reason; he knew no one even remotely associated with that bank, and could not recall having heard the name in conversation or having read it somewhere at some time. So much for Felicity Bank. It wasn't his bank here in Hong Kong, and he doubted it ever would be.

He lit a cigarette then and pondered the paradox of George Winch, ex-bureaucrat, extortionist, and permanently retired— to the best of his knowledge—on some desolate, God-foresaken little prison island off the Argentine coast, convicted of a number of crimes against the state, chief among them of accepting and passing counterfeit money, consorting with undesirable characters, and of murder. It had been Angel Tanjeloff, the undesirable character and maker of counterfeit bills, who had been murdered. Tanjeloff had been a murderer himself, besides one of the top racketeers in Argentina whose death let several high-ranking government and military officials off his many hooks. Gratitude should have been forthcoming to Señor Jorge Winch from all parties concerned, but Winch, unlike Tanjeloff, had nothing on anyone, so it must have seemed the most expedient thing to do to just consign him to prison and chance his death at the hands of the most vicious criminals apprehended in Argentina. Bad luck for a first offender.

Who else could know about Winch and Tanjeloff? If Winch were still living . . . No, thought Fury, it was unlikely that Winch had the wherewithal for a long pursuit. And if the authorities had wrested the truth from Winch, it also seemed unlikely that they'd have waited this long to do anything about it. In fact, it was implausible that they'd even care what was the truth or not.

The truth was that Fury had killed Tanjeloff—who had murdered a valued business associate—then had blackmailed Winch, who had tried his own brand of extortion—money for import licenses—into taking credit for the racketeer's death. And Fury left the country, two years ago, for the last time with the money which both men had tried to relieve him of.

So whoever had the gumption to drop Winch's name as part of a "somewhat curious prank" must know everything there was to know about that affair. But who? And for what purpose?

Finished with the *Post,* Fury put it aside and suddenly wanted to look at the *Commodities Quotation,* a morning commercial paper that would have this morning's prices. He went to the bedroom and rang up the concierge for one to be sent up.

"We are sorry, sir, but the *Quotation* is not yet available. We understand their delivery truck had an accident on its way here." Before he could say thank you anyway, the voice on the other end continued hurriedly, "Was there any particular item you were interested in, sir? We can quickly consult our market service."

"All right, then," he said. "Would you have sent up a list of the local tungsten quotes—Oh, a sample spread from opening bell to now?" He knew what they'd do: send a complete list of both stock and commodity quotes and prices from the Hong Kong, Singapore, Tokyo, Taipei and Manila exchanges, plus yesterday's late New York figures. There was no limiting these people.

"Of course. In ten minutes, sir."

"Thank you. Just have it put on the nightstand."

"Will that be all, sir?"

"Yes, thank you, that's all."

He hung up, then stretched, glancing at his watch. Ten-thirty. Tungsten might have moved a whole quarter point in either direction since the city's exchanges opened an hour and a half ago. Or not at all. It was that kind of commodity. Basically inert. He had one last sip of coffee, extinguished his cigarette, then strode briskly to the shower.

When he emerged again the breakfast cart was gone, the room tidied up, and a computerized list there on the nightstand. He picked it up, scanned it, then exclaimed silently. Tungsten had shot up just over ten points, opening at the bell two points higher than he had ever known it to be. He turned the list over and noted the date-time stamp: ten-thirty-eight. He glanced over the four Hong Kong exchange columns. Several tungsten stocks had advanced just as spectacularly. But in Tokyo, while the futures were way up, the stocks had plummeted. Singapore showed mixed reactions, but it was activity where there had been none before, not to his memory. Taipei duplicated Singapore, while Australian and New Zealand stocks *and* futures had gone through the ceiling. Manila showed nothing; a hand-written note in that column explained that the government had devalued the peso and ordered all banks and exchanges closed this morning.

He put the list down and finished the knot of his tie. The phone jangled then. He picked it up. "Yes?"

"Merritt?" inquired a bouncy Australian voice on the other end.

"Derek!" smiled Fury, sitting on the edge of the bed. "You found me."

The voice on the other end laughed. "Where else? You and the Mandarin are married. Two o'clock at Ushio's?"

"Fine. Everybody here?"

"All present. Get in last night?"

"Midnight. How's business?"

"Top drawer. Brought some nice pelts with me. Yours?"

"Fine. Derek, what's with our metal?"

"Someone mistreating it?"

"I don't know. Bluelist must be on fire. All Asian tungsten is up. Don't know if it's done the same in New York or Chicago, or even London. Couldn't look at a *Quotation*."

"Let me look. By the by, what did you bring?"

"Chocolates."

"Bonne chance, chap! Briscoe isn't into luxuries. See you at two!"

"See you, Derek," said Fury, replacing the receiver. He rose, slipped into his jacket, and quickly surveyed himself in the full-length mirror. The light blue, light-weight suit wore like air, an important advantage if one wanted to beat Hong Kong's high humidity. A midnight blue, crocheted square-bottom tie on a white cotton shirt, one of the few whites he owned. He noted the changes in his features. His brow looked and felt lighter, his green eyes were relaxed, absent of all former caution and annoyance, and the skin of his face had exchanged the tension of necessity for the tension of unabridged, unopposed purpose. Being in Hong Kong did that for him every time.

After one last tug at the tie, Fury collected his briefcase and left the suite.

Neither he nor the young elevator operator was prepared for what confronted them when the doors rolled open in the lobby. There was a crowd of people waiting, the chatter of hundreds of voices, and flashbulbs going off like silent fireworks. For a second, no one noticed the elevator; all attention was centered on a little man in a dark suit who was trying to make a statement in painfully broken English and numerous hand gestures to a scribbling, open-mouthed Western newsman. He was Chinese, perhaps fifty, with a smooth, glossy face under a sweep of thin white hair. He was surrounded by a bevy of younger, similarly dressed men, all of them facing the pressing crowd, watching, scowling at the flashing cameras. In the crowd were other journalists, the khaki of the Hong Kong Police, plainclothesmen, curious guests, and stiff, enduring, self-conscious older gentlemen in pinstriped suits who seemed to huddle close to the little man lest they be forgotten.

An instant later all heads turned automatically to the elevator. As he walked out, Fury's eyes met those of the little man, which were dark, hard, marble eyes, seeming to accuse Fury of prolonging his discomfiture in the lobby by having dared use the elevator. The impatience of death was in those eyes.

Their eyes met and froze for an instant more, and then the little man brushed by Fury, followed closely by the older gentlemen, half a dozen of the young watchers, and then by a line of police, who planted themselves in front of the open elevator doors. Everybody tried to follow.

As Fury shouldered his way through the crowd, someone gripped his elbow. It was the hotel manager. "Sorry about that, sir," he shouted into Fury's ear, "but we weren't expecting him so soon, or we should have had a lift set aside for him."

The manager, a tall blond man in a tuxedo, waved his arm and made a path for them through the inert crowd of on-lookers. They wound up underneath the enormous, futuristic chandelier of glass and crystal that was the centerpiece of the Mandarin's lobby. "No damage, I hope," laughed the manager as they both straightened out their jackets. "We don't carry riot insurance here."

"I'm fine," said Fury, grinning. "What was that? A retired Kung-Fu star?"

The manager laughed again. "Oh, no," he said. "That was Lon Ping. He picked one of our meeting rooms upstairs for a conference with the Council."

"Who or what is Lon Ping?"

"He arrived yesterday. Our observer without portfolio in Hong Kong for the People's Republic of China. The first! Took everyone by surprise, including us! We had *no* idea that it had been decided to have one. Thought that was years away. Well," said the manager, taking Fury's hand hurriedly and pumping it twice, "can't chat. Won't happen again! I might be needed upstairs! Good day!"

Fury watched him vanish into the throng, then turned and went to the desk, where he changed a traveler's check into Hong Kong dollars and change. He was busy stuffing the notes into his wallet when he suddenly sensed that he was being watched. He turned his head and met the almond eyes of an auburn-haired Eurasian woman just a few feet away from him down the counter. The woman turned and spoke to the clerk about her mail. Pepper gray blazer with a red insignia on the breast pocket, gray skirt, white blouse, maroon ascot. Rich, brown hair. Damned good-looking, he thought.

He shook the incident out of his mind and walked to the nearby public phone. "Tinto? . . . Fury here. . . . Hello. . . . Have time for me? . . . No, not over the phone, too long a list. . . . I was on my way over but thought I'd better call first. . . . See you then. . . . "

He took a taxi to Des Voeux Road Central and called on the offices of Grosset, Hill & Tinto, custom manufacturing brokers and export consultants.

Ronald Tinto, an ex-commissariat officer of the Royal Marines who had been with Admiral Harcourt during the re-occupation of Hong Kong in 1945 and who had stayed on after his discharge, rose and offered his hand when the secretary let Fury in. His silky white hair contrasted sharply with Fury's black. He wore no coat in the un-air-conditioned office, but some personal code of decorum dictated that he wear his shirtsleeves down with cufflinks in place. "How are you, Merritt?" he greeted as they shook hands.

"Never better. Yourself?"

"Outrageously content. Have a seat," he gestured, following suit. "What can I do you for this time?"

"Who's good for hand calculator components?"

Tinto waved his hands. "That depends on which components."

"Basic memories," said Fury, opening his briefcase and consulting a note pad. "Specifically, part BX-21421G, Cochran's Standard Parts Catalog."

"I see," murmured Tinto, jotting it down, then swiveling his chair around and picking out a copy of the catalog from the shelf behind him. He flipped through it and stopped at a page that was covered with his own notations. "Yes, yes . . . Well, you have several choices, Merritt. There's Oriental Electronics in Kowloon, Wells-Millan Electronics, Kowloon, and Rapid Technologies, New Kowloon. Who's your customer?" he asked, looking up again.

"A department store chain on the West Coast. High quality goods, sterling name, premium prices. They've contracted a California assembler. Not interested in marginal stuff. Their money-back guarantee staff has never been more than two people for the whole chain and they want to keep it that way."

"Got you. Then I recommend Rapid Technologies. Run by a work horse, Paul Chan. Know him well. Used to be a busboy at the Imperial Hotel. Done a lot of the Japanese name brands and they sing his praises. How much and when?"

"Ten thousand units by the end of January."

"That's a goodish order," beamed Tinto, jotting it down.

"I'd like to see the plant and take back a few samples for the assembler to play with."

"I'll call Chan and see if he's game. Let you know by the end of the day. Where are you staying and for how long?"

"The Mandarin, two weeks. Any day is fine. Open schedule."

"To whom do I charge my exorbitant fee?"

"Bluelist, my account. You have the number?"

"In my files. Next item?" asked Tinto, turning a page in his own note pad.

"Cigarette cases, leather and plastic."

"Wait," said Tinto, holding up a hand. "Have you much more?"

"Loads."

"Then why don't we have tea over it?"

"Fine," said Fury, taking out his cigarettes and lighter.

Before he left Tinto's office an hour and a half later, tungsten was the least of Fury's concerns. When he returned to Kai Tak airport again in two weeks' time, he would be taking with him delivery contracts for electronic components, cigarette cases, standard typewriter ribbons, cassette tapes, playing cards, camera lenses, and ladies' lingerie. All bound for the States. It meant half a year's work ahead of him to guarantee those deliveries, and if all went right with production and shipping, he stood to collect over a quarter of a million dollars in commissions.

Tinto would collect a percentage of that commission for his work, and a higher percentage than Fury might have paid to other consultants in Hong Kong, but he found Tinto to be much more knowledgeable and discriminating in his choices of businesses and manufacturers than others he had used in the past. There were excellent, average and bad concerns in Hong Kong, and Tinto, having been here since the end of the war to see it change from a strictly entrepot warehouse port to a major Far East manufacturing center, knew them all.

Fury stood outside Tinto's office building on Des Voeux. He had an hour before the meeting at Ushio's.

He was very much tempted to walk Des Voeux back to his hotel half a mile away. The swift crowds of people, the bustle and clatter of the trolleys, double-decker buses, taxis and mini-buses, the rumble of movement and purposes and goals, the soaring towers of granite and concrete and the racket of more going up, all struck a sweet, seductive note in his blood that was pure exhilaration. He lit a cigarette to measure the time he would permit himself to walk, then took a step and let himself be carried away by the throngs.

He checked at the hotel newsstand for the *Commodity Quotation;* their stock was in. He purchased one and headed for the Clipper Lounge, where he could have a cool drink, a coffee, and time to recompose himself before taking a taxi to the meeting. He gave a cursory look at the prices, wanting only to verify the tungsten activity. Then, certain that some bit of news had touched it off, he scanned every news item in the paper.

He found it on page ten, in just over an inch of print, so dwarfed by an engineering firm's three-quarter page ad calling for subcontractors' bids for a sewage project in Jakarta, that he almost missed it:

> Washington (21 Oct.)—The Senate
> Subcommittee on Strategic Materials issued
> a paper yesterday recommending the impo-

sition of price ceilings on domestically produced tungsten, accelerated government stockpiling of the processed ore, and the reduction of all tariffs and duties on its importation. Concurrently, Senators Upton Bookin of Idaho and Martin Denning of Rhode Island, both members of the sub-committee, announced the pending introduction in the Senate of a bill which would incorporate the study's conclusions. 'We are entering an era in which we think it wise to increase our dependency on outside sources for this vital material,' Senator Bookin was quoted as saying, 'not only because we shouldn't squander what little we have, but because we are going to have to import it in the future anyway.' Senator Denning added: 'Voluntary integration into the world economy is imperative if the U.S. is going to share in the task of helping raise disadvantaged but politically unattractive nations by their bootstraps into active, prosperous participants in world peace. It's simply a matter of short-circuiting envy: people wouldn't commit crimes if they had just as much as others. There's that, and there's the obvious fact that it's a good conservation measure.' The Senators did not indicate the chances of success for the bill in either the Senate or the House.

The paper slipped from Fury's fingers and flopped to the low table at his feet. That was it. His next thought was: That's the end of Bluelist Tungsten Trading.

熊市場

Chapter 3

Windfall

The Bluelist Tungsten Trading Company, Ltd., was not in business to mine tungsten, but to serve as a convenience for its partners. It mined tungsten, but very little of it, from a very small hole in the ground near Cloudy Hill in the New Territories. It earned enough income to pay to have it mined and to partly offset the partners' various government-incurred overheads in the course of doing business in other parts of the Far East.

Fury had only just returned from an expedition to the States to find something to import into Hong Kong, something that would earn Bluelist even more income and which would effectively reduce their collective overhead to zero. All of the partners—including Fury—were very active and constantly increasing both their own incomes and their claims on the common account, into which went most of Bluelist's tungsten earnings. Each partner had a separate account with Bluelist and every contract or commission he made was made in Bluelist's name. Any and all overhead was charged to the common account, and there was very little it could sustain any longer. There none restrictions or taxes on anything that was imported to Hong Kong or exported, so the "overhead" scheme could work even with a marginal money-maker.

Bluelist had been the idea of one Sir Harry Grampian Briscoe. One morning over a year ago Fury walked into his small import-export office in New York and found in the mail an invitation from Briscoe to ". . . take advantage of the incomparable opportunities of the Colony of Hong Kong entrepot and manufacturing market. I am seeking a limited number of partners, individuals already experienced in international trade, who desire a more convenient and livelier base of operations and an arguably more sympathetic environment from which to conduct trade. I have recently purchased a minimal-production mine in the adjacent New Territories. This mine, originally called Blue-list No. 4, is to be the root base of a new venture by which, with the combined finances of other partners, I admittedly hope to reduce my own liabilities and operating expenditures. Such a base would similarly benefit other partners, preferably those with American dollar assets, by means of a reduction in bank and brokerage costs which the natural advantage of a partnership/general trading company has over individual enterprises. . . ."

The letter seemed legitimate enough to Fury. How an international trader on the other side of the world had heard of him, Fury had not the faintest idea. Perhaps some mutual business acquaintance had referred Briscoe to him.

But Hong Kong intrigued him. He was just then winding down his South American business and was looking for something to supplement his European trade. The magic of Hong Kong and its free port, its efficient banking system, and the prospect of tapping the lucrative West Coast markets beckoned to his instincts. He answered the letter.

Two weeks later he met Derek Speake, a fur trader from Australia and already a partner in Bluelist, under a Remington painting in the Rough Rider Room restaurant in the Biltmore Hotel. Speake was in New York for a fur auction and a merchandising show. He was a big, gaunt, blond man from

Sydney, ten years Fury's senior, with such an infectious, out-going manner that he made anyone he met think he was living in the best of worlds.

Fury, too well acquainted with the sales techniques and showmanship of con men, judged Speake to be *bona fide,* original and refreshing—after a quick phone call to a garment district furrier, who informed Fury that Speake was one of the best suppliers he had.

And so Derek Speake sold Fury on Bluelist. Speake had the papers with him; Fury signed them, and handed him a bonded check for twenty thousand dollars, the price of a junior part-nership, plus a statement of value, a statement of assets, and a list of trading interests.

A month later Fury met his partners:

Sir Harry Grampian Briscoe, O.B.E., K.C.M.G., D.S.O., Army Colonel Retired, a London banker who left for Hong Kong and became one of the biggest dealers in Malay lumber and bamboo in the Far East. He also dealt in Indonesian tobacco, Australian and South African coal, and—it was rumored—gold bullion;

See Pok, a Chinese refugee who now owned a Singapore shipbuilding and repair yard, a Singapore bank, and several Hong Kong banks, and was part-owner of a Japanese trading company and wholesale outlet;

Walter Pelosi, an American from San Francisco who spe-cialized in purchasing Hong Kong toys and home decorations for American department stores;

Bernardo Ronquillo, a Manila trader who specialized in sand and cement;

Jumpei Ushio, head of a medium-sized Tokyo trading company which dealt in anything, and whose company both operated the mine and bought most of its output.

Briscoe and See Pok had provided the majority funds for Bluelist Tungsten Trading, but it was Briscoe who dominated the company. The man fascinated Fury. He was a tall, trim, fit man in his late fifties or early sixties, very active, very efficient in his speech and manners, but the thing that most commanded anyone's attention was his face. There were handsome faces and ugly faces and faces one never noticed; Fury might have called Briscoe ugly if Briscoe were less a man. It was a wide, expansive face whose bone-structure was more noticeable than any of its other features, which seemed to have been stuck on as an afterthought. Recessed and almost lost in the deep, wide sockets were aqua-blue eyes, divided an inch and a half on either side by a small, insignificant nose. A massive brow melted into a reduced crop of flaxen, perpetually neat hair; it might have been done in porcelain. There was very little chin under a normal but disproportionate mouth, and over it a long, thin moustache which Fury guessed Briscoe grew to visually connect the two sides. But it was the kind of face Fury could see running through the hyper-competitive, fortune-strewn Far East market, a face meant to give orders and to take delivery on them, the kind of ruthless, dogged, daring face that might have wrested the barren island of Hong Kong from the fishermen villagers who had first inhabited it, and defied the Imperial war junks sent by Peking to take it back.

Fury had no time to know any of the men on more intimate terms than as partners. They met quarterly in Ushio's offices to take stock of how well the company was doing. Fury did not see Hong Kong as much as the others. He was busy in the States amassing a fortune—one aided invaluably by working out of Hong Kong—which would allow him to run through the States. Bluelist's "overhead" scheme saved him tens of thousands of dollars that might have been lost forever to American import duties. It was the best business relationship he had experienced to date.

Until now. Sitting alone in the Clipper Lounge, oblivious to the chatter of the lunchtimers around him, he was unsure of how news of the tungsten bill would be received by Briscoe and the rest. He felt certain that one or more of the partners would want to do something, even though it was clear that there was nothing to be done. He hoped Briscoe took a firm grip on the matter and vetoed any nonsense. If that did not happen, Fury committed himself to selling his interest in the company.

He glanced at his watch: thirty-five minutes to go. He decided to have a quick lunch, freshen up a bit, then leave for Ushio's. With one last look at the article, he folded up the paper, put it in his briefcase, stood up and left.

*   *   *   *   *

Ushio's offices were in a commercial building between Jaffe and Lockhart Roads in the Wanchai district, only ten taxi minutes away. When he arrived, only Speake was there, going over his account with a bookkeeper. After they had shaken hands, Fury asked him if he had seen the *Quotation* item. "Haven't had any time to think about it, lad. Been here since noon with Miki here, trying to run down a check I should have got from a fur dresser here two months ago. Conference room's open and tea's on the table. Go on in and collect your thoughts. Miki has your books all set to go over after the word war."

"Thought you hadn't any time to think about it," smiled Fury.

"At the moment, I'm more concerned about the money I've lost than the money I'll lose."

They came in one by one. Ronquillo arrived first, shook hands with Fury, then plunked his briefcase down on the table. Fury slid the *Quotation* down the polished top of bare walnut to him, open to the circled item. Ronquillo read it through, looked at Fury, and asked, *"Pare,* these *Yanquis* are no relatives of yours, I pray?" Ronquillo, forty-five, a big swarthy Filippino of mixed Catalan and Moorish features, flashed a broad, sad smile at him.

"By neither blood nor brains," answered Fury.

Ronquillo tapped the item with a finger. "This will cost us Bluelist," he said. "Our little anthill will become too valuable, and then we will squander it."

"Agreed," said Fury, lighting a cigarette. "But you seem to have gotten it from both ends," he added, referring to the devaluation.

Ronquillo shook his head, amused. "Half my money is in Singapore and half here, divided between twenty banks and this soon-to-expire company. I keep nothing of value in that crazy country."

Next to walk in was Walter Pelosi. He was a man whom Fury would never have noticed on the street, a medium-sized man, probably fifty, with black thinning hair, black plastic-rimmed glasses, and a tan that would not take, not even with lotions. He wore an expensive but drab brown suit. On one lapel was pinned a tiny round emblem that identified him as a member of the Optimists Club; on the other was a small plastic American flag. He was the only partner who seemed out of place in the company. Fury always expected him to be very active and vocal and brimming with jokes and ideas; Pelosi had sat back very seriously in all their past meetings and perhaps uttered twenty words the whole time. Fury could form no opinion of him, except that he did not fit his idea of a savvy Far East trader. But then, he thought, they came in all shapes and sizes.

Pelosi strode in briskly and deposited his gray Samsonite briefcase on the table. "Morning, gentlemen! Fantastic day, isn't it?"

"Good afternoon, Walter," said Fury. "Have you seen this?" he asked, handing Pelosi the paper.

Pelosi took it, glanced at the article, then beamed joyfully. "Heh! How about that! Manna from heaven, huh?"

"That's debatable," replied Fury, taking the paper back.

Pelosi frowned. "Why?"

He had no chance to explain. See Pok came in then, followed by Speake, Ushio, and finally Briscoe. There was a brief round of greetings and handshaking. Fury showed Briscoe the article. With some relief to Fury, Briscoe nodded immediately in apparent recognition of it and wrung his mouth distastefully. "They do lay the humanitarianism on a bit thick, don't they? Fool politicians. Don't worry, Merritt. We'll be tossing this about today."

Briscoe sat at the other end of the long table. On his right was See Pok, on his left Pelosi. Speake, Ronquillo and Ushio were in the middle. Fury sat at the other end, facing Briscoe. See Pok was the oldest present, perhaps sixty or sixty-five. Far from being dry and withered, he was a spry, light-footed man with dimples and a faded twinkle in his eye. He wore steel-rimmed glasses, and his white hair, still thick and abundant, was done in a crew-cut.

Jumpei Ushio was the only man who came close to Fury's age, about thirty. He was the archetype of the modern Japanese entrepreneur: young, enthusiastic, articulate in three languages, hard-dealing.

Briscoe wasted no time in opening the meeting. He stood up and said, "Without a doubt, gentlemen, the market fluctuation of tungsten as inspired by certain events in the American congress is foremost in everyone's mind here. However, I have no inclination to allow the intentions of Senators Denning and Bookin to dictate the order of our concerns. I'm sure we are all much more interested in what Merritt has brought us from Babylon." Briscoe smiled with a nod to Fury and took his seat.

Fury put his briefcase in front of him and opened it. "These," he said, and took out several flat, rectangular white-wrapped bars of chocolate and slid them down the table to each man. "For the general market in Hong Kong. Plain West German chocolate. Or Dutch. Or American. Bought by Bluelist as you see them. If we buy in Europe we can have them wrapped in Kansas City Duty Free and sent on here, or sent direct from Europe and wrapped here. The cost differences are minimal any way one looks at them because we can sell to retailers at a one- to two-hundred percent mark-up and still offer a bargain. We can introduce plain chocolate for a start, come out with almonds and bitters later. What to name it?" Fury shrugged. "Blue Mountain Bars, Blue Luck, Blue Lake, whatever; an ad agency here could better think of the right name and design a wrapper besides." He paused. "Or—we could sell at cost, let someone else put his name on it, and take a commission. However we work it we stand to make half a million Crown dollars a year on not much of a volume, one hundred thousand of that clear profit, which is more than enough to cover the Bluelist common account."

The men had all opened the bars and were munching on them—everyone except See Pok, who sat with his hands folded, listening to Fury with a fascinated look on his face, and Pelosi, who was leaned back far in his chair, staring disdainfully at the bar in front of him.

Fury smiled, and took out several sheets of paper. "Here are the facts and figures," he continued, passing them around. "They tell the whole story. If we're all agreed, it would mean an initial investment of ten thousand per partner, which could be repaid within four months. Jumpei's company could handle the whole operation for a higher percentage of the profits." Fury returned to his place at the table. "One phone call from me to the States could have the first shipment here inside of two weeks." He took his seat and lit another cigarette.

"Short and sweet," chuckled Briscoe. All the men laughed. Briscoe took out a pair of reading glasses and scanned the sheet in front of him. There was silence in the room as they all read the proposal. "Offhand," said Briscoe at last, looking at everyone over the tops of his glasses, "I can't see anything objectionable to the idea." He laid the paper down and removed his glasses. "Does anyone here see anything sour in Merritt's choc-olate scheme? He certainly has done his homework."

No one objected, though Fury did notice that See Pok studied the sheet with an air of detached formality, and Pelosi with languid boredom. Derek Speake smiled at Fury. "Top of the mark," he said, turning then to Briscoe. "I'll cast my cash in it, Harry."

"Bernardo?" asked Briscoe.

Ronquillo shook his head, saying, "I find no fault. I am willing. We will need it more than ever now."

Briscoe looked to Ushio, who gestured briefly with his hand. "I concur with Señor Ronquillo. Bluelist of old is finished now."

"Walter?"

Pelosi tossed the sheet on the table. "I'm game if the rest of you are," he replied with a doleful sigh, looking up.

Pok glanced at Fury; his eyes twinkled with tentative admiration. "Technically feasible," he commented.

Briscoe slapped his hand on the table lightly. "Done, then! Unanimous vote of confidence for calories and cavities!"

This caused laughter around the table, joined by everyone but Fury. Something unexpectedly raw in Briscoe's manner stung his mind, to which he replied mentally, silently: Don't be facetious, Harry.

"Congratulations, Merritt," said Briscoe. "But hold off on that phone call a while, would you? We're going to discuss general business now, then wade into the tungsten matter."

"Fine," said Fury. "Just as long as I can make it before the end of the week."

"What is today?" asked Briscoe, glancing at his watch.

"Monday. The end of tomorrow would do, eh?"

Just then the door opened and one of Ushio's secretaries looked in and exchanged words with him. The secretary disappeared and Ushio stood up. With a faint bow he said, "Excuse me, gentlemen, but my home office is calling with urgent business. Please continue without me, as I do not know how long I will be. Many apologies."

When Ushio was gone, Briscoe sighed, more with relief than distraction, noted Fury. In a small way, it prepared him for what happened when everybody was finished reciting the state of his business and what he looked forward to in the future.

Ushio had not yet returned half an hour later when Briscoe said, "I know there are certain of us here who have reservations about the Bookin-Denning bill announced in the press this morning. I would, however, like to hear them from your own mouths first before I proceed on this subject. Bernardo?"

Ronquillo shrugged. "If it were not for Merritt's proposal, Señor Briscoe, I would be obliged to withdraw from Bluelist. The short-term benefits of this—if the bill becomes law—would destroy the purpose of our partnership, which is to save money, not make it, by the limited graces of our mine."

"Walter?"

Pelosi sat forward and grinned at them. "Windfall!" he exclaimed with enthusiasm.

"Derek?"

"I must go along with Bernardo, Harry," said Speake, casually lighting a pipe. "If tungsten goes up, that mine will be gone inside of four months. I'll stay in provided we find another scheme for a common account. Merritt's has the makings of that. Besides, we *can* make money on that scheme. All we need to do is alter the articles of the partnership to distribute the profits."

Briscoe looked to Pok.

"I see nothing to excite negative sentiment," pronounced the old man.

"Merritt?"

"I concur with Derek and Bernardo, Harry," said Fury. "And I think that when Jumpei returns, he most of all would be able to quell any enthusiasm about the 'windfall' nature of our property."

"Perhaps," said Briscoe. He took out a gold cigarette case and took his time lighting one of the oval tubes he took from it. After two contemplative puffs on it, he sat back and said, "See and I had a little talk this morning, gentlemen. And after protracted deliberation on this morning's news, we reached a mutual decision. We want you all to know that this development in Washington has inspired See and me to submit to Jumpei that his firm increase the production of the mine in six months' time. We have tentatively contracted a Japanese firm of Jumpei's acquaintance to expand and modernize the present ore refining facilities near the mine. Further, See here has generously offered to sell to Bluelist at an attractive discount a large capacity, sea-going freighter presently being completed in one of his Singapore yards. The vehicle for this purchase will be an equally attractive loan from Felicity Bank on Jordan Road, Kowloon, in which Mr. Pok has been recently installed as co-chairman and treasurer."

There was a silence at the table. Finally, Speake said, "We're speechless, Harry."

"Does Jumpei know your decision?" asked Fury.

Briscoe smiled. "Not yet he doesn't."

"We cannot afford it," shrugged Ronquillo incomprehensibly.

Pok leaned forward. "Can we afford not to afford it?" he asked. "This is a golden opportunity. I can assure you all that other firms are this very minute formulating similar options and plans."

Ronquillo held out his hands in exasperation. "Señor Pok," he explained slowly, painfully, "with all due respect to your eminence in financial things, I must point out that Bluelist Number Four's output is not worth the purchase of a . . . a rowboat, much less a sea-going freighter. I doubt if we could fill the captain's cabin with our monthly production. And there is another thing," he continued, pointing his finger at the air in general, "a *very* important thing. There is no guarantee that this American nonsense will become law. How many laws and controls such as this one are chewed up by factions in the American congress and die? And the American president can veto it, too. Let us not forget any of these things."

"They'll pass it, Bernardo," said Briscoe with the conde-scension he might have reserved for a child. "In some form or another, they'll pass it. I'm confident enough in my literacy in these matters that I can assert that the American mining lobby was more surprised by the announcement than any of us. There wasn't a breath of forewarning about it anywhere— apparently."

"We'll petition the Queen to award you a garter for your literacy in these matters, Harry," said Speake with his own brand of indulgence. "I'm sure you deserve one. However, it still doesn't clear up the matter of how it could concern or benefit us in the least. It amounts to our holding a few soggy matches at the sudden decree of match rationing," he chuckled ironically.

"See and I differ," answered Briscoe.

Pelosi said, "And if you see differently, Derek, you can get the hell out!"

Briscoe looked sharply at Pelosi. "None of that, Walter. I won't tolerate that kind of tone in my company." Pelosi twisted his mouth and stared at the table. Briscoe looked to Fury. "Have you anything to say, Merritt? You're always good for a laugh."

But no one laughed. Something new had taken over here, thought Fury. Something—he could not quite put his finger on it—was at work here intended to drive the members into two different camps. He asked, "What do you know that we don't, Harry?"

"What do *you* know, Merritt?"

"That you couldn't fill a tenth of the hold of the smallest freighter with all the raw ore from Bluelist. That at the expanded production rate which you and See propose the mine would be exhausted within four to six months. That we are fortunate that the ore is rich enough in tungsten that Jumpei doesn't need to work the mine six days a week. That it will last two or three years more with his sending out a crew three days a week, as he has been doing."

"That's what you know?"

"It's known by all of us, Harry. In fact, all my points made up your key selling point on the whole mining scheme."

"You're absolutely right, Merritt," said Briscoe. "But—we've discovered otherwise since then. You're not a mining expert, anyway."

"No, I'm not. I'd like to hear what Jumpei has to say about your idea." He tried, but failed to hold Briscoe's eyes. They coyly avoided his own.

"We can wait until he comes back," said Briscoe with an easy smile. "But I'm sure he'll disagree, too. With *you*, that is. To continue—See and I anticipated differences of opinion. The only one who's shown any agreement with us has been Walter here. Our tungsten expansion would necessitate an additional—and substantial—financial commitment from each and every one of us. See and I hold majority interests in this company and we're both solid enough in our outside interests to go it alone or together. However, we do invite your participation. But in the regrettable event none of you wants to join with us, we're quite willing to suspend a paragraph or two of the incorporation papers and buy your interest."

Speake and Ronquillo stared at Briscoe unbelievingly. Fury shook his head and ground the stub of his cigarette in his ashtray. "Harry: It *can't* work."

"You *are* persistent," remarked Briscoe, his smile weak.

Speake said, "Harry, the plant that's out there now has never even been opened. It just isn't worth the return. A more efficient plant such as you propose would only make matters worse."

"Really?"

Fury said, "So we don't stand to gain from what the price ceilings on American mines will do—close down the marginals there—do we? *We* are a marginal, Harry."

Briscoe waved his cigarette hand. "There are lapsed mines all over the New Territories, Merritt, and on both sides of Tolo Channel. Their leases should be easy to pick up."

Speake sighed and sat back, defeated. Fury went on. "Any one of them is worth less than Bluelist. We'd lose money if they cost us nothing to re-open."

"Correction, Merritt. What you say may be true, but I anticipate demand to be such that it *will* be worth our while to re-open any one of them. Or *all* of them. And aren't you forgetting something else? We can lease the new refinery to other producers. Malaysia, Indonesia, the Philippines—they all export tungsten."

Ronquillo laughed. Fury shook his head again. "Together they produce less than we do. The big producers are Bolivia, Peru, Brazil, Argentina. And those are all state-run mines. The States has never had to depend on their output because it's been able to produce most of what industry needs there and import the rest on its own terms—on market terms."

"Back to this side of the world," said Briscoe. "True, Malaysia and Indonesia don't produce much. So it wouldn't be practical for them to build processing plants, when they can use *ours. That's* what we have in mind, Merritt. Then, there's Australia, and New Zealand. Especially New Zealand. They have a fabulous scheelite deposit on the South Island, you know. I really envy the company that owns that tract in these circumstances."

"They can build their own plant on-site, *and* their own port. I know the site you're talking about. It's six thousand miles south of here, and you're grasping for straws, Harry."

"And I would remind you, Harry," interjected Speake, "that Australia harbors the same species of koala bear as does the States. Once the mining unions there catch wind of the new tungsten market, they'll abort any expanded Australian production by demanding a cut of the profits. You can count Australia out."

"And more," continued Fury. "Have you any idea what these ceilings are going to do to the price of steel? Tungsten's an important alloy—especially for metal-cutting tools in heavy industry—so you can expect price increases all around. And what will they do to the cost of lighting fixtures in the States and in Hong Kong? The States could absorb some of the price hike, but Hong Kong couldn't. Dozens of marginals will close here and tens of thousands lose their jobs. This is a form of inflation, Harry. No good can come from it. Your expenses at the mine will increase and they'll have increased wherever you turn. So this bill really isn't the gift you think it is."

Briscoe regarded Fury for a moment. "Thank you, Merritt, for the lesson in elementary economics. You missed your calling, you know." Before Fury could respond to his sarcasm, Briscoe then threw up his hands. "I've *never* seen so much opposition to a windfall!" he exclaimed.

"I'm all for it, Harry!" said Pelosi, jumping up and glaring at Fury. "Goddamn, nothing better could have happened! Look, Merritt, these birds in Washington are always going to be playing around with one thing or another, and there's nothing we can do about it! We may as well rake it in when it comes our way, take advantage of it! Use your head, Merritt!"

Pelosi's behavior was too odd for Fury, and he was tired of it. "Mr. Pelosi," he began in the most formal tone he knew, "many girls in Hong Kong will be assaulted between now and tomorrow morning. Very pretty girls, too, at just the right age. It's going to happen; someone is going to do it. You may as well get your licks in, too, Walter. It's going to happen anyway."

Pelosi's face reddened, and the man just stared at Fury, his mouth open.

"Don't be morbid," reprimanded Briscoe.

"Am I being any more so than you about your proposition for Bluelist?"

See Pok rose abruptly. "When cooler heads deign to sit at this table, I shall return." He picked up his briefcase and walked out.

Pelosi bent and retrieved his briefcase. "Me, too! I didn't come here to listen to sick jokes!" He stormed out after Pok.

Speake looked around. "Well, I'd say this meeting was adjourned, Harry."

"Yes," replied Briscoe, his eyes on Fury. "I agree. We may as well break here as any time else. We'll sit again at four, what?"

Speake rose. "I'll tell the others, Harry. Tea, Bernardo, Merritt?"

Ronquillo rose in silent affirmation. Fury shook his head. "Not now, Derek. I'm going to go over my accounts with Miki."

"Okay, see you at four—or earlier, if you can."

Speake and Ronquillo went out, Speake shaking his head at Fury out of Briscoe's sight. Briscoe took out another of his oval cigarettes and tapped it on the flat case several times, then broke his stare at Fury to light it. Twin jets of smoke shot out from his small nose, and a cloud obscured his eyes as he said, "You *can* be grit in people's teeth, Merritt."

"It's been my life story," said Fury.

The smoke rose and cleared. Briscoe's deep eyes were still fixed on Fury. "Do you desire to remain in this partnership?"

"I haven't decided," said Fury. "It's still an interesting arrangement."

"Then I suggest that you drop your opposition to our plans for the mine. And that you apologize to Mr. Pelosi for your insinuative remarks on his character."

Briscoe's tone—that of a father admonishing a son—grated against Fury's sensibilities; he knew Briscoe had said it that way in a last effort to set them apart, though what his purpose was he couldn't imagine. Fury said, "You and See, Harry—you seemed well prepared for an event that took even the insiders by surprise."

Briscoe waved his cigarette hand in dismissal of the observation. "See and I took the liberty of drawing up those options shortly after this firm was founded, Merritt. We are essentially men of action, and we *were* prepared."

Fury shut his briefcase. Briscoe continued. "Now: we're split down the middle on this matter. We can't go on that way. Ronquillo might be persuaded. Walter is gung-ho. Ushio may be amenable—once he learns what I know and you don't; *he* probably stands to make more on this development than any one of us. Derek? Well, I know Derek. He's out. You, Merritt? You're one of the few knowns—there's no persuading you. I realize that more deeply than you."

"I'll find out sooner or later, Harry," said Fury. "What *do* you know? What makes you think it could work? And what makes you willing to use the kind of tactic you used here, one obviously designed to break up the partnership?"

"Bolivia? Brazil? Argentina? Exporters? They're nothing, Merritt. But don't concern yourself. You say it can't work. Act on your assumption. Get out."

Fury smiled, shook his head and stood up. "All the evidence says you're wrong, Harry. You haven't countered a single objection of mine, yet you're convinced you're right. It makes me wonder why."

Briscoe looked up at him through another cloud of smoke. "It's a big world, Merritt. We'll have another go at it in the near future. All right?"

"If you wish," said Fury.

"Most earnestly," smiled Briscoe.

風吹果落

Chapter 4

Nothing
But
Solitude

There was nothing left to do at the Bluelist offices. He spent fifteen minutes checking his record against Miki's, Bluelist's accountant, for outstanding bills and credits, found everything in order and up to date, and initialed Miki's chit sheet. He decided there was nothing to be gained by going back to the meeting at four. He'd only be pressed by Briscoe for a decision and he wanted time to think. If he went to the meeting, tempers were bound to flare again. Pok was right.

So he left. On his way out he checked Ushio's office; his secretary said he was still on long-distance and not likely to be free for half an hour. He passed the company library where Speake and Ronquillo were having tea. "Not coming back?" queried Speake.

"Not today," said Fury. "There'd only be another row, and I'm expecting calls at the hotel."

"I'll drop by later," said Speake. "Have anything planned for this evening?"

"Nothing but solitude, but I'm open to suggestions."

"Merritt," said Ronquillo, "you have just come from him:

how is Briscoe?"

"Bull-headed and determined to do exactly what you think he's doing," replied Fury.

He needed time to think, so he walked back to his hotel. It had all happened so suddenly. What the hell was Briscoe trying to pull? What could he possibly gain by deliberately alienating his partners by virtually kicking them out of the company? Well, not all of them. Pok was for the expansion plan, and so was Pelosi, but their behavior didn't add up to anything he could comprehend, either. Cold water, hot water. No, he thought; Pelosi's actions were in character. He knew Pelosi least of all. They had talked shop on occasion but Walter never seemed to be that interested in either Fury's business or his own. But he suddenly comes to life at the oddest moment! That fact kept returning to Fury's mind and confounded his repeated efforts to make sense out of what had happened.

He stopped and lit a cigarette outside the building, forcing the puzzle to the back of his mind. It was still a paradox and he'd go mad if he followed it around in circles. Let it simmer on a back-burner for a while, he told himself. Clear your mind of it, let it grow distant, then approach it from a fresh angle. There simply wasn't enough information to work with.

He took Lockhart Road back, strolling leisurely to allow the feel of the meeting to melt away. The street was a canyon of ten- to twenty-story buildings, a mixture of offices and tower factories that were unique to Hong Kong and which turned out so much of its exports. Ushio's building was typical; an outside corridor from the pavement led to a bank of elevators, and on either side of it were glass advertising cages and see-through ground-floor shops. Taken together, it was a run-riot combination of the *gallerias* of Buenos Aires and the long arcades of London; one could spend an entire afternoon on half a block of Lockhart alone and visit but a fraction of the shops.

Fury stepped into a calculator shop and came out ten minutes later with a Rapid Technologies pocket model. The proprietor enthusiastically endorsed it as one of the best made. But he would endorse anything with enthusiasm, Fury thought with amusement.

Somewhere between O'Brien and Luard Roads another sign caught his eye: Dragon Double Six Bookshop—*Secondhand Books of the Finest Quality and Lowest Prices.* In the dusty windows were piles of old paperbacks, clothbounds and stacks of the inevitable British picture books. And centered in between a pile of red Baedekers and a six-volume history of Burmese art was a three-volume collected works of Frederick Schiller, in English, obviously a well-preserved nineteenth century edition. Fury turned into the street-front shop.

He asked the proprietor—an old Chinaman in a white suit and burgundy tie—for the books, and when he had examined them, found that they were in almost mint condition, opened perhaps once in their lifetime. The embossed leather spines had not one scratch or blur of mold on them, the sewn binding was stiff yet still supple, and every page of the 25-pound paper was intact, with only traces of yellow and brown near the gilt edges. Even the red ribbon place-mark had survived, still silky and full of spring. The publisher—Moorland & Steptoe, Covent Garden, London, 1848—eluded his memory, though. He looked up at the proprietor. "Do you know publishers?" he asked.

"Yes," answered the Chinaman. "You do not recognize Moorland & Steptoe?"

Fury smiled. "No," he said, "and I don't want to buy a bad translation, either."

The old man shook his head in assurance. "Moorland & Steptoe—one of the finest publishing firms of the last century. Specialized in German literature. Went out of business during the Great War, in 1916. Very ironic. An incendiary bomb dropped from a raiding Zeppelin fell on their building, destroying it and killing half the company's employees."

"What was so ironic about that?"

The old man shook his head. "They were working on a special encyclopedia of German music for the British Museum. Ten years of effort went to the winds."

"Then I must agree that it was ironic," said Fury. "You certainly know your publishers."

"Better subjects than people."

Fury wasn't interested in that kind of conversation. He merely smiled in answer, put the Schiller volumes on the counter, and turned to browse. Most of the books were in Chinese, tens of thousands of them, but there was a separate section of dusty shelves near the door reserved for "Foreign Language" books. It was an eclectic collection, mostly in English, ranging from brittle, yellowing war-issue automatic arms manuals issued by the Defence Ministry to a Draper's *Intellectual Development of Europe* to a Raymond Chandler anthology to a curious little turn-of-the-century volume called *The Taxes on Knowledge,* which turned out to be a history of the British newspaper industry.

Then he spotted a thin, two-year-old edition of *The Far East Directory of Business and Commercial Leaders.* He took it down and leafed through it, looking for Briscoe's name. There it was, at the top of a four-inch entry, too long to read here. He glanced at the price in the front: two dollars. He decided to take it, and reached also for two of the arms manuals. He owned two automatics in the States; he could take them apart to clean and put them back together again, but when he bought them they came without ownership manuals because those particular models were outlawed by the Treasury Department.

Outside the shop he shifted his packages to the other arm

and glanced at his watch: time to go back to the hotel. Tinto may have called by now. He walked to the corner and hailed one of the ubiquitous Mercedes taxis.

*   *   *   *   *

He showered, changed into slacks, a blue Lacoste shirt and slippers, then called the concierge and asked for the London *Financial Times* and the *Asian Wall Street Journal;* the desk said that no calls had come in for him while he was out; if Tinto was going to call today he may as well catch up on some reading while he was waiting. He was fixing a drink at the sidebar when the papers came. At last, he settled comfortably in a chair by a window in the sitting room with the drink, papers and phone on the table beside him, and opened the *Directory.*

Briscoe never talked about himself, not even to his closest associates. Fury shared that reticence with him. And what little he knew about Briscoe had been mentioned in the query he had received over a year ago. It had never occurred to Fury to wonder about the rest of the man, or about his past. Briscoe had been so compelling a personality in his role as a Far East trader that he had accepted the man at face value; being accepted that way with no questions asked was also something he shared with Briscoe.

O.B.E., K.C.M.G., D.S.O., Army Colonel (2nd Battalion, Northumberland Light Infantry), Special Forces Group 9, Detached Service with Allied Control Commission, Vienna; discharged, returned to Cambridge, Master's in economics; officer, Regency Road Bank, London; second delegate, European Economic Conference; senior delegate, European Currency Assembly; author, White Paper on "Regional Economic Administration and Autonomy," for the Foreign Office; knighted; founder, Asian Ways Construction Materials & Trading Company, Hong Kong; occasional consultant to the

Executive Council of the Colony. . . .

Well, that fleshed things out a bit, thought Fury, putting the open book aside and lighting a cigarette. Briscoe. Wealthy family, Harrow education, little scholar with "firsts" or honors in everything he touched; then two years at Cambridge before taking a commission to see the world in the worst possible way—from both ends of a gun. What had he done to win a colonelcy, wondered Fury. That "Special Forces Group 9" had a vague, classified ring to it. And the knighthood and the other awards: What had he done to earn them?

See Pok. *He* should be in here, thought Fury, reaching for the *Directory* again. Yes, he was, but the entry was only an inch long and said nothing about Pok that was new to Fury. There was no mention of Felicity Bank; the directory predated its founding.

He snapped the book shut and took a sip of the drink to cap a new thought: What in God's name did Briscoe need *him* for? Or, for that matter, any of the others?

The phone jangled then. Fury finished the drink and picked up the receiver. It was Briscoe.

"Sorry about the tiff we had, Merritt," he said smoothly over the musical chimes of an antique clock in his study. Fury recognized them well, and checked his watch with a frown: four-forty-five. Damned short meeting, he thought. "If we're still on speaking terms, may I stand you lunch tomorrow? I think we might iron out our differences in more amicable circumstances."

Fury asked, "With the others?"

"No, just you and I. And maybe See. The others are all going to be busy."

"Okay, Harry," sighed Fury. "But I can't guarantee any ironing."

"Whatever. We'll just give it another go and see what happens. Would twelve noon suit you?"

"Yes, I'm free then."

"Wonderful. Do you know the Gorgon's Head in the Sai Ying?"

"I'll find it, Harry. I can't talk any longer. I'm expecting calls."

"No problem, Merritt. We'll talk enough tomorrow. Good day."

Fury hung up and glanced at his watch again. It must have been a *very* short meeting. Well, what else was there to discuss? He reached for the *Asian WSJ* and settled back in the chair.

Fifteen minutes later he was in the middle of an article on a new technique for cotton irrigation being tried in Australia, when Tinto called. He had three appointments for him the day after tomorrow for the calculator parts, the camera lenses and the ladies' lingerie. The companies were open to commit themselves, said Tinto, and he suspected that all that really remained was the settling of the terms.

"Felicity Bank, Tinto," broached Fury after jotting down the appointment information. "What do you know about it?"

"The basics," said Tinto. "Why do you ask?"

Fury explained the tungsten expansion scheme and Pok's role in it.

"Not quite two years old," said the broker. "British funds, Chinese management, local business. Brainchild of a London banking syndicate, the Houghton-Devane Group. I'm surprised, too, Merritt. I don't see any returns on that scheme at all."

"Is Regency Road Bank in this syndicate?"

"Why, yes, they are. Odd," mused Tinto, suddenly fascinated by this aspect. "Regency Road is such a mite of an establishment. Any of the other members in that syndicate pay out in interest per annum the reported assets of Regency. Yes, that *is* odd," he added. "If firms go the syndicate route they usually keep to their own size. What brought up Regency Road?"

"Oh, I'm just looking into why's and wherefore's and that name strayed along," answered Fury. "Pok: I know his basics, too, but can you give me your rendition?"

Tinto seemed to shrug over the line. "I know very little about Mr. Pok. His yards built some of the freighters out in the harbor now, he holds a few banking positions here besides Felicity, and he *owns* an investment bank in Singapore by the name of Key Commercial. . . . I read somewhere that he was one of the three-quarter million Chinese who flocked to the Colony in 1949 after Mao ran his flag up in Peking."

"No," sighed Fury, "there's nothing new there, either."

"Let me know the outcome, will you, Merritt?" said Tinto. "Sounds like you and Briscoe will be at loggerheads over this for a while. I want to know where to send my bills."

Fury laughed. "Send them to Bluelist until further notice. Talk with you tomorrow, Tinto. Thanks."

He managed to finish the irrigation article and was opening the *Times* when the phone rang again. "Come on up," he said to Speake, who was calling from the desk downstairs. "I know you have gossip."

"I'm here to invite you to dinner this evening at the restaurant of my choice," said Speake when Fury let him in. "Have a bit of celebrating to do, I do. Game?"

"Tux or business?" asked Fury, going to the side bar.

"Tux," said Speake. "I'll have a wee Bloody Mary, thank you. Have a tux?"

"No, but they can fit me one here and have it ready in two hours," said Fury, handing Speake his drink. "What's the occasion?" he asked, reaching for the phone.

"Call the tailor first," said Speake, taking the chair opposite Fury's.

Fury was told that a fitter would be up in fifteen minutes. He sat down and leaned back.

Speake said, "Bluelist: I'm out of it."

Fury gestured in toast with his drink. "I thought so," he said, sipping the drink. "I may do the same."

"Wait for Harry to break the ice, though. He offered me one and a half times my interest. Could have had twice or even three times that and a few other goodies, but I didn't feel like bickering, I was so disgusted."

"He's already approached me," said Fury. "I'm meeting him for lunch tomorrow." Fury paused. "Why did you sell, Derek?"

Speake shrugged. "Basically, your objections are mine, Merritt. I can't see us making anything out of that legislation. Perhaps there's gold or manganese in the mine that Harry knows of, but if Harry knew it, so would Jumpei, and Jumpei would have told us."

Fury cocked his head. "Would he have?"

Speake nodded. "Yes, he would have told us." He paused with a sigh. "No, there's something else about it I don't like. Easy charity. Too easy. So I'm pulling out to keep my copy-book clean." He paused again. "Ronquillo's out of it."

Fury gestured with the glass again. "He has enough troubles as it is."

"True. One and a half again."

Fury sat forward. "You don't smell anything specific, Derek?"

"I do, lad, but I can't place it. Never saw anything like this before. Just can't put a tag on it, you know? A man like Briscoe—he can't have come this far placing bad bets like this." Speake took a swallow of his drink. "Ready for the next fatality?"

"Who?" asked Fury, frowning.

"Jumpei."

"Jumpei?? But he operates the mine!"

Speake rose and began pacing in front of Fury. "Enter Pok," he said, "who suddenly announces that his trading outfit can do the job more cheaply—as though Jumpei had been lavishing brass lanterns and air-conditioning on the mine! Briscoe points out that there's a rider in the incorporation papers that allows the company to juggle operations at its discretion for economic reasons—which means it can run off and rip up operating contracts as it pleases. There was that bomb, but first came the news—news to Jumpei—that Bluelist was going to expand. Jumpei laughed right in Harry's face. He knows that mine better than any of us."

Fury simply stared at Speake, amazed.

"And to sweeten the deal," continued the Australian, "Briscoe offered him a guaranteed percentage on the stepped-up production. Jumpei asked him if his wits were on holiday, and added that he may as well be offering him one of the rings of Saturn. But Briscoe wasn't in so affable a mood and Jumpei soon took it to heart. Ever hear an extended session of Japanese invective? Jumpei threw up his hands in the end and hit the phone for headquarters."

Fury was silent for a moment, thinking. "Pok's outfit: You wouldn't happen to know what it does through Bluelist, would you?"

"Why, yes," chuckled Speake, sitting down again. "Luggage and office supplies. We were all quite surprised that it had a mine engineering and geologist staff, let me tell you!" He set down his glass, and took out a pipe and tobacco pouch. "What do you suppose they're up to, Briscoe and Pok?" he asked, packing the pipe.

"They want to be alone," mused Fury, half seriously. "Pelosi: was he there, too?"

Speake grinned. "Can't say. He just sat on the sidelines and took notes. Which is more than *he's* ever done for Bluelist. Miki says he doesn't take that many toys out of here."

"I wonder how Briscoe and Pok would take it if I decided to stay in?"

"Can't rightly say, lad. Though when we reconvened minus your temperizing presence, Harry made light of your chocolate scheme. Said Bluelist was in a different match now and fee on your chocolates."

Fury took one last swallow of his drink. "Think about the whole meeting, Derek. Doesn't Briscoe's conduct of the meeting strike you as schizophrenic?"

"Bingo, lad!" replied Speake. "A basket case! You have a hunch?"

"A very frightening one, Derek."

"What?"

Fury shook his head. "I'm not certain yet. I'll let you know when I put *my* tag on it. There are such things as slander laws." He smiled and slapped his hands on his knees. "Enough of Briscoe for a while. What about this dinner of yours?"

Speake grinned. "Know a nice French place in Kowloon. *La Lumière à la Fin du Monde.* We meet there at eight."

Fury moved his lips silently, translating it in his mind. "The light at the end of the world," he said. "Suits Hong Kong."

"Doesn't it, though? I hope the young lady I selected as your companion suits you as well."

"What young lady?"

There was a knock on the door. As Fury went to answer it, Speake said, "You don't think I'm going alone there with you, do you? It isn't exactly a fish-'n'-chips stop, *ma Lumière.* I'm going to be spending a packet tonight on four places and the least I ask is that two of them be blessed by skirts."

Fury let the tailor and his assistant in. The tailor offered Fury a small catalog of styles. As he browsed through it, the tailor went to work with his measuring tape and Speake continued. "The lady I have in mind is a fabulous hourglass I met at an official to-do last May. 36-24-36 o'clock."

Fury grinned as he leafed through the pages. "Statistics can be fascinating but are often quite meaningless, Derek."

"She's a secretary of something at Government House."

Fury shook his head. "Distinctly not a recommendation."

"This one has a degree in economics from London University," said Speake. "A high octane lady in many respects."

Fury indicated one of the styles to the assistant, who made a note of it on his pad. The tailor then began dictating. "Derek, let me pick my own company," said Fury, dropping the catalog on the coffee table.

"Where are you going to find someone on such short notice?"

"I noticed plenty of women down in the Lounge, and probably they *all* love French restaurants."

Speake shook his head. "No, no, Merritt. You've never gone out here. You don't know the protocol. Leave it to me. I vouch for this one. I bore her stiff, but you might be her cup of tea."

"You're selling again, Derek," chuckled Fury.

"Damn right. Give it a ride, Merritt. She's a Hong Kong Booster."

Fury looked at him dubiously as the tailor measured his waist.

"Trust me," added Speake.

"Said the Walrus to the Oysters. Or was it to the Carpenter? All right, Derek," said Fury, as the tailor double-checked his measurements of the shoulders, "sign her on for a blind date. I need to clear my head anyway."

"You won't regret it, Merritt. You'll thank me some day."

When everyone had gone, Fury pulled up a chair facing the window and sat for an hour or so, relaxing for the first real time since he woke up this morning. The window faced east, and he could see what counted. Kowloon on the peninsula, to the north across the harbor, basically flat up to the short range of small mountains which practically encircled it. Kowloon was growing as Hong Kong proper could not; it reminded him of a compacted Los Angeles, a sprawl of lower buildings dotted with taller structures. Below him, Victoria—or Hong Kong—struck him as a stylized San Francisco, a forest of granite, concrete, sheer towers swelling abruptly up from the harbor's edge to encrust the sides of steep thousand-foot masses, refusing to be dominated by them.

New York was his favorite city; he planned to make it his headquarters some day. Hong Kong was his only alternative choice. True, he thought, the ways of the outside world were encroaching on the spirit of Hong Kong and causing its marvelous gears to strip here and there; and Hong Kong's chances of surviving a mere fraction of the political, arbitrary nonsense borne by New York and London and all the other great commercial centers were much less in that it was the last civilized outpost in a portion of the world which was growing more and more barbarous. It could go only so far along that destructive, suicidal route; free trade and everything else that it implied made it possible; one had it, or one didn't. There was no in-between here, there was nowhere else to go, except to the water, or back to China.

He'd read that when Hong Kong's New Territories reverted to Peking's sovereignty near the end of the century, Peking might permit things to remain as they were now. Possibly, thought Fury. Peking was already very much active in Hong Kong's markets. When the reversion took effect, there would be only Kowloon and the Hong Kong Islands left, mere finger-holds under the boot of a continent. Peking valued Hong Kong as a source of hard currency and trade—as a window on the world of values. But it couldn't have Hong Kong and rule it at the same time; that was an issue and conflict only power-hungry bureaucrats wrestled with. Peking would destroy Hong Kong, and the last enduring jewel of a much vandalized and much apologized-for crown would twinkle out forever.

Or Hong Kong would destroy Peking.

Hong Kong *was* a colony, though it wasn't considered good

form to call it that these days; the word incited propaganda outbursts from local leftists and Peking, and caused tired, apprehensive men to wince with imagined guilt. Hong Kong was a colony of reason, and always had been, whether it thrived under the protection of the Union Jack, or under the colors of a flag that had never been sewn—and might never be.

Fury was not optimistic about the colony's future. It was, after all, a sparkling exception to the rule, a many-faceted jewel fixed in the path of a cancerous nightmare. Few men had the courage to defend it even now. There would be nobody to defend it at the end of the century. St. George had already traded his armor for St. Augustine's burlap sack and was preaching self-denial to everybody but the dragon.

Fury watched the eastern sky grow pink. The mountains were beginning to turn dark, and below him the first lights of the city and harbor were appearing. Rapidly the pink flushed to red. He drew harder on the cigarette in his fingers, causing the fire to burn brighter. "Tungsten," he said to himself, quietly.

除了孤寂，一無所有

Chapter 5

The Light at the End of the World

La Lumière à la Fin du Monde was on Printing House Close, an alley just off Nathan Road, the busy stretch of light that ran from the Star Ferry Terminal on the water to the mountains of the New Territories. Fury, in a rented MGB, drove casually along Nathan. Its neon was in full glory now, a vibrant, exciting blend of pinks, blues and greens on white and black mattes. There was something appealing about Far East night lights, he observed, something unique in the way neon colors were used here. There was none of the tawdry garishness of senseless contrast so common in the West. It was as though the principles of Oriental painting had been successfully applied to commercial advertising.

The restaurant was in a clean, shrubbery-planted alley in an old factory building, on top of which was a huge billboard featuring a bobbing forearm and a digital watch and a single line of copy that read, "The only moving part of this watch is you—Wing Ting Clocks." The watch face flashed on: 7:59. Below, over a modest facade of glass doors, black-onyx marble pillars and white brick, blazed a neon torch, rippling in waves of blue and white. An old Chinese doorman in the uniform of a Paris *gendarme* blew his whistle; an attendant appeared and Fury gave him the car keys.

The Australian was waiting in the crowded anteroom. "They'll be late," he said. "Amber had some rush work thrown on her at the last minute. Won't even have time to dress as I had hoped she would. Annette's picking her up and they're taxi-ing over together."

"Annette and Amber—who's who?" asked Fury as they sat down on a leather couch.

"Annette Hitchings. Lady my age from my parts. Went to primary school with her in Sydney. Used to put worms and things down the back of her dress and she'd get back by putting dirt and things down my socks. Runs a fashion model-ing agency here now. We still bedevil each other, though we're past the worm and dirt phase. She's a redhead; she isn't yours." Speake paused as he and Fury accepted aperitifs from a hostess. "Amber? Amber Lee," said Speake with a dreamy affection.

"Tell me something about her."

"I won't tell you much. Might take the punch out of the pleasure and kill conversation. She's a one-and-only between East and West. Father: Horatio Marlborough Lee, the Gover-nor's physician for years until he retired from the civil service to start his own practice among the millionaires here. Mother: Lan Kei—better known as Lavender Lan, one of the most respected and sought-after professional 'consorts' in Hong Kong ages ago. Ran a spy ring for us during the occupation and did in a few Japanese officers, too. She probably would have gone the Madam route if Lee hadn't met her one lonely evening and decided to take her out of circulation. Genuine match. Both dead now, buried side by side in the Catholic cemetery near Happy Valley Race Course. Which is fitting, since they both made a fortune on the fillies."

"And Amber?" asked Fury.

"That's all," smiled Speake. "Ask me about the restaurant here. I'll tell you anything you want to know."

Fury glanced at him suspiciously. "Why are you being so secretive?"

Speake shook his head. "Host's privilege. Not to worry, though. No one's ever complained about my blind dates. I enjoy arranging them. It's a real art, bringing couples together. Tests my judgment of people. Might have been a marriage broker, or a boxing referee."

Fury laughed. "All right—what about the restaurant?"

"Chicken any way imaginable. Boneless, basted, barbecued, boiled in oil. Your heart's craving, their specialty. I think this is the only restaurant in town that hasn't a single entree of seafood on the menu."

The place was obviously a favorite with Hong Kong's wealthiest, best known, and best-mannered inhabitants, a strictly white tie and jacket-evening gown establishment. Most of the staff, Fury observed, spoke French as well as Chinese and English. There the "Frenchness" of the place ended. From where they sat he could see into one of the four, twenty-table dining rooms, this one done in late eighteenth century neoclassical decor, with sky blue walls and ceilings with white pillars and moldings, furnished with Sheraton and Chippendale pieces.

The arched niches in the walls were the least French of all. Usually they contained Greek or Roman statuary. In these instead were white marble statues of historical Hong Kong personages: busts of two English traders of the early nineteenth century, the names Jardine and Matheson carved into the pedestals; a Blackwatch officer in full regimentals, brandishing an authentic claymore broadsword; a Royal Marine; a British merchant seaman; an old Chinese banker in traditional costume, contemplating a dish of gold taels, or tiny inch-square bars; a Chinese pirate, ready with a wickedly curved sword and a wheellock pistol; a petite, graceful Chinese maiden, nude, apparently crouched over a brook, admiring her reflection.

Fury was sure that the gold taels *were* gold—silver-alloyed gold. And he supposed the maiden was inspired by the sprite of White Rock Club Soda labels.

"Yes," said Speake, "they *are* gold, in case you're wondering. And they're safe enough here. The owner has a security agreement with the Domino Triad, the straightest secret society in the colony, that if one of those taels is ever missing—there are fourteen of them—the Triad must replace it at its own expense. Which is no little task, since bullion is banned here, at least for Europeans it is. The owner gets away with it because the bars are for display only. 'Part of the art,' he says. They've been there for twenty years, ever since he opened this place. The authorities were a bit more genial back then. How *he* got a hold of them is no little mystery, either. But, to my knowledge, those bars have never been touched."

Fury looked around, then chuckled, "What security, Derek?"

Speake nodded to a passing maitre'd. "Oh, I'd venture to guess that not quite all of the male staff are Domino members. Bouncers and armed guards are quite superfluous here. Just look at those bars the wrong way and your waiter is as easily capable of breaking your neck as serving you your second course."

Speake was sitting facing the entrance. His face suddenly lit up. "Ah, here they are!"

He and Fury rose. Fury saw Annette Hitchings first as the women threaded their way through the crowd. She was a tall, lithe, vivacious redhead in her late forties, and her black gown caused heads to turn.

Then both women emerged, and Fury grinned in recognition of Amber Lee. It was the woman who had been watching him in the hotel. Their eyes met in mutual surprise; she was just as startled to see him.

She was Eurasian, with her features weighted on the Caucasian side. Wide cheekbones angled up from a grim, full mouth to capture a slender European nose and wide, almond eyes, which were curiously more Slavic in slant than Oriental. Her face was barely oval, made less so by high, arching eyebrows. Her shoulder-length hair was auburn and curly, her skin the shade of burnished peach. He liked what she did for her face—almost nothing, except for some rouge and lipstick, and perhaps a touch of eyebrow pencil. It was a beautiful, exotic face. And there was no trace of the inscrutable he had seen in it earlier in the day. She held his glance and waited. She wore what he had seen her in earlier, the black blazer ensemble, with a large, wide purse slung from her shoulder.

And when she turned her head during Speake's introductions, he caught the oddest, most alluring thing about her: in a certain light, her eyes flickered yellow, like a cat's in the dark; it was only a brief flickering, like a single revolution of a police car's flasher. He ascribed it to some unusual pigmentation in the iris.

"Derek," cooed Annette Hitchings as she appraised Fury with frank, pleased eyes, "when you said you were bringing an associate with you tonight I wouldn't have imagined it could be anyone under forty."

"The table is this way, my dear," replied Speake, taking her elbow and steering her away, "and at which you can insult me at your leisure."

Fury offered his arm to Amber Lee. "You won't have the disadvantage of distance now, Miss Lee."

She grasped his arm. "Nor you, Mr. Fury."

Speake's proposed table plate of chicken in red wine, and chocolate mousse was accepted. Light piano music drifted in from one of the other rooms, encouraging nothing but the most casual conversation. Fury sat opposite Amber; the light of the candles on the table shimmered ominously on the Chinese pirate that seemed to stand protectively above her. Talk centered around Speake's fur business, and then Miss Hitchings' modeling agency, which, Fury learned as a silent guest, had branches in Singapore, Sydney, Tokyo and Taipei. Amber joined in the conversation.

In time the conversation turned to Fury, the only stranger. "Have you been in the Far East long, Mr. Fury?" asked Miss Hitchings.

"Not long enough," said Fury. "Just over a year."

"There's something about you, dear. You seem to be too young to be in the company of my old flame Derek here. How old are you, if you don't mind my asking?"

"Twenty-nine."

Miss Hitchings leaned forward and curled a sleek hand under her chin. "Goodness, Mr. Fury, shouldn't you be home smoking pot and listening to some incoherent rock album by the 'Graphic Arts' or some other oddly named group, or sitting in a park drinking bottles and bottles of beer and just generally making an untouchable nuisance of yourself? You seem to be out of step with your generation."

Fury shrugged. "Accident of affiliation, Miss Hitchings. I avoid packs."

"But you seem much older, though. Mature, I mean. I usually think of men your age as boys."

Fury smiled uncomfortably. He disliked talking about himself. "I was fortunate enough to be socially and culturally deprived at a very early age."

"Have you any schooling or family?"

"None that mattered," answered Fury, twirling the stem of his brandy glass between his fingers.

Speake sensed Fury's reluctance and made an attempt to rescue him. "Annette, love, why must you worry the lad with so many questions? Isn't it obvious he doesn't fit his generation?

I don't think his appearance is the crucial difference, in which case we're not here in this lovely, very expensive place to discuss the general decline in taste and decorum or the value gap between Merritt and his contemporaries."

"You *are* refreshing, Mr. Fury," persisted Miss Hitchings. "I really must invite you to lunch some time when Derek is away peddling pelts. I'd get your life story *then*."

Speake winked at Amber, who sat watching Fury with a faint smile on her lips. "Give Amber a chance to coax it out of him," he said.

"But he's so attractive," said Miss Hitchings, deliberately gauging her words to tease Speake, "isn't he, Amber? And your kind of man, too; basically silent and very stingy in the private sphere. Mr. Fury, I ought to invite you to one of my shows some time and plant you at the end of the runway. The sight of you down there might put more sass into my girls when they're showing off Derek's goods."

"Weren't you complaining earlier that your girls are too stiff, Annette?" asked Amber. She took a sip of her brandy, then smiled at Fury. "I rather think he'd frighten them."

"Mr. Fury doesn't frighten you, surely?" laughed Miss Hitchings.

"No."

Miss Hitchings sat back and raised her eyebrows. Speake broke in before she could say anything more. "Annette, dear, they're playing a nice waltz in the other room," he said, rising and taking her hand. "Why don't we take advantage of it and let these two take advantage of our absence, eh?"

When they were gone, Amber reached into her purse and drew out a cigarette. Fury lit it. Her eyes reflected the flame of his lighter. "Thank you," she said, exhaling.

"My pleasure," said Fury. He added, with mock seriousness, "I'm not often that civil with civil servants."

"Oh? Why not?"

"They get in my way and make my life too expensive."

"Am I costing you anything?"

"That depends on what you do."

She smiled at him strangely. "I supervise the economic section in Colonial Administration. We collect economic data, do surveys, issue reports for the Development Council."

"Derek said you have an economics degree from London University."

"Yes. My parents—they're both dead—left me more money than I could use. That's how I used it."

"Do you enjoy your work?"

She flashed that strange smile again, which never quite vanished. "Enormously."

"Why are you called Amber?"

"Do you think it an odd name?"

"It's enchanting."

"My eyes."

"Your eyes?"

"Yes. They glint amber in the right light. Like a cat's."

Fury chuckled. "I made the same observation. Your parents had imagination."

"Actually, it's an Arabic name, but they didn't know that when I was born. The doctor who delivered me noticed my eyes while the nurse was washing me off. He commented on it to my mother, and she decided to call me Amber." She paused. "Do you like working with Derek?"

"We've never worked together."

"I don't understand. Annette said you and Derek were partners."

Fury shook his head. "We are, but Derek trades only in furs. I deal in anything that might make money. But—he's leaving the partnership, and so might I."

"Which partnership?"

"Bluelist Tungsten Trading." Fury paused to light another

cigarette. "What were you doing in the lobby of the Mandarin this morning, besides watching me?"

Amber took a sip of her drink, then looked up and smiled. "Covering the arrival of Lon Ping," she answered with too straight a face.

"Why would Government House send an economist?"

Amber raised her eyebrows diffidently. "Shortage of staff."

Fury didn't believe her answer. "And what was your interest in me?"

"You're an interesting man, Mr. Fury. You should be used to women looking at you."

"Not quite the way you were, as though I were a suspect who needed watching," he chuckled. "You're certain you're not really with the Hong Kong police?"

Amber smiled pointedly. "I'm sure, Mr. Fury," she said. "Though you're not."

He narrowed his eyes. "I'm certain that you called me early this morning claiming to have a telegram from one George Winch," he countered. "I know there should be only one person in the world who would understand the meaning of that name enough to use it. Me."

"You're beginning to sound mysterious, Mr. Fury. What *does* that name mean?"

"You tell me."

Amber shook her head. "Certainty can be one of the most tenuous footholds in life, Mr. Fury. You should be extra careful about where you step."

Fury finished his brandy. "And I have many mottos, Miss Lee. One of them is 'Don't tread on me.' Quite a few men failed to heed that motto. They wound up wishing they had been more literate."

"Such as George Winch?"

"Especially George Winch." Fury paused. "I've never had to remind a woman of it, though."

Amber studied his stern face and seemed to be pleased with it. "And *I'm* sure that not so many women bother you who need to be reminded. Except Miss Hitchings," she added with a chuckle.

"And you," said Fury, holding her eyes.

The smile disappeared and she averted his glance for a moment. When she looked back up from her drink, she asked, "Bluelist Tungsten: isn't it Sir Harry Briscoe?"

"Yes. Do you know of him?"

"We . . . met at an official gathering once. In fact, at the same one where Derek and I met. He introduced me to Briscoe. Why are you leaving a partnership with *him?* He is one of the most prominent businessmen in Hong Kong—in this part of the world. Nothing he does fails."

Fury shrugged. "He's senior partner with another gentleman and they insist that some asinine behavior on the part of some American politicians will make them money. I disagree. So does Derek."

Amber studied her cigarette. He loved the way she looked then. "What particular asinine behavior are you speaking of, Mr. Fury?"

Fury spoke with tired, bored irony. "Two civil servants—in collusion with a committee of them—have decided to preserve the country's tungsten by pricing it off the market. They want to make it impossible for anyone there to mine it."

"Isn't it an important steel alloy?" she asked. "How do they expect American steelmakers to produce without it?"

Fury shrugged again. "I don't know. They mentioned lowering tungsten import tariffs. At any rate, steel prices will go up if they make their desires law. I imagine the quotes for long-term orders have already gone up from fright."

Amber frowned. "Yes, they have, somewhat. I saw some American quotes just this morning. I couldn't understand why." She studied her cigarette again. "And I can't understand why Briscoe thinks. . . ." Her sentence trailed off.

Fury poured himself another brandy. "Well, I don't think I'll sell out until I know what Briscoe's up to. I have plenty of time for that."

Amber smiled pleasantly at him. "How long do you plan to stay in Hong Kong?"

"Long enough to collect a dozen or so delivery contracts for my import business in New York."

"Do you enjoy *your* work?"

"Enormously," he laughed.

"Do you like Hong Kong?"

"I love Hong Kong."

Amber frowned. "Everybody says that. All those gawking tourists. They'd say the same thing about their mothers-in-law's pot roasts. *Why* do you love Hong Kong?"

"It bears a striking resemblance to what I imagine my country used to be like. Turn-of-the-century New York and London in one package. Business-wise, I'm more at home here, I think, than any place else on earth. I . . . belong here."

"With the sweatshops and the low wages and the dangerous working conditions and the total lack of job security?" she taunted.

"I've been through all that and worse," he said. "There's an electric parts factory in Long Island City—just across the river from Manhattan, alongside some very noisy elevated subway tracks. It met all of your aforementioned specifications, besides being located in one of the more dangerous parts of the city. I lied about my age to work there; I was fourteen when I started and sixteen when I left. I screwed parts together, spliced wire, and split insulation for two and a half years."

Fury paused, and seemed to forget Amber. "I left there each day for another full-time job as a waiter in a hotel restaurant in Brooklyn, from six to midnight. It wasn't so much a restaurant as it was a pit-stop for syndicate underlings. I found the cockroaches better company than most of the people who sat at my counter those nights. Both jobs were hot, tedious, and physically and mentally exhausting. And every night I would go home to a dingy, vermin-ridden room that measured eight feet by sixteen. It was on the West Side, on an avenue close to the Hudson, a heavy trucking artery. I rarely noticed the rumbling and shaking, except when I left in the mornings and came home at nights, or when I just lay awake, thinking, and planning."

"You make it sound worth remembering," said Amber. "So grim and joyless a childhood."

"No, not grim, nor joyless," smiled Fury. "Not one moment of it. Hard, and sometimes impossible and discouraging, but not grim."

"Others would be bitter."

"Yes, I suppose they would," said Fury. "At the end of three years I'd saved enough to buy several dealer's lots of gold coins, which, after another year, I banked into enough money and credit to buy and import a large consignment of Swiss precision, temperature-controlled mantle clocks, which sold well in the dearer department stores. That made possible . . . everything else that's followed since. It's been a matter of geometric progression, in a manner of speaking."

He saw something sly in her expression. "Perhaps others like shoveling coal and spinning yarn and screwing things together on an assembly line. Perhaps others can't share your attitude because they have no ambition. Perhaps they do not think a lack of ambition is a crime. Do you presume the right to look down on them?"

This time Fury frowned, not sure of the intent of her question. He shook his head. "Dead-ends are for deadbeats. I shed no tears for inertia." Then he chuckled. "Are you satisfied now that I'm not just a token admirer of Hong Kong?"

Her eyes narrowed. "Would you die for it?"

He thought about it for a moment. It was a good question. She had asked it too lightly for him to give it a snap answer. "If it . . . were the light at the end of the world, yes, I think I would," he said finally. "But it isn't. The States is."

"And why would you be willing to die for *it?*"

"Because if *that* goes, there'd be no room for me. Or anyone like me. Anywhere. But—I don't think I'd die. I'd stick around and make a nuisance of myself."

With a toss of her hair Amber abruptly dismissed the subject. "I'm curious: How did you ever come to associate with Sir Harry Briscoe?"

Fury told her about the letter and Speake.

"You're a strange man," she said suddenly.

"I've been called worse," smiled Fury.

"And I know you better than you think. Give me your hand."

Amused, he obliged. She held it open, palm up, and studied it for a moment. Then she intoned, almost as though to herself, "You are a man at odds with the world." She casually ran the finger of her other hand lightly from the hump of his thumb to his middle finger, then traced the lines in his palm, saying, "A man who will not be stopped. It is your destiny— no, your choice—to be alone, solitary, intact. You are vital and alive. You see corruption and stupidity and malignancy in the world, and you will not be part of it. You will have your way, or the world will have you in a way it would rather not contemplate. You will be hated by many, loved by a few, unknown to most. You justify nothing that is your own, for you know its source, while others weep for the food in their mouths. You are one, they are many, and so the gods smile upon you. It will always be so—with you."

Fury angrily clutched her finger in a tight grip. "That's nonsense, what you're doing."

"What am I doing?" smiled Amber, making no effort to

extract her finger.

"Palm reading."

"You don't believe in it?"

"There are more plausible systems for winning on the stock market and the racetrack, and they're nonsense, too."

"I know. But what I said is true, isn't it?"

Fury considered the open, almost amused look in her eyes, and felt her finger slip away. "If you know that much, you'd also know that I don't acknowledge compliments as lavish as the one you've just thrown. I expect to be taken at face value."

"Which for you *is* a compliment, and one, I'm sure, very rarely paid."

Fury could only smile and sign in defeat.

"Did I bother you?" she asked.

He glanced lingeringly at her ascot, noticing the way the folds breathed almost imperceptibly with her bosom. "You know damned well you did." He put out his cigarette. "And I think it's too much of a coincidence, your being here tonight."

Amber shook her head. "No. Derek really invited me. He . . . told me about you some time ago."

"I have an idea," said Fury, reaching for the decanter and pouring them both another glass of brandy, "that we would have met eventually anyway. I smell designs. So I'm warning you: I don't like being used. By anyone, for any reason."

"I know, Mr. Fury." She picked up her glass and held it out for a toast, studying him, the contour of his face, his body. "Here's to you," she said, "and to all my designs."

"Bonne chance, milady," smiled Fury, touching his glass to hers.

Then they drank.

Fury put his glass down and shifted in his chair. What was happening was happening too fast. He said, "Derek and Miss Hitchings have been away a long time."

"They're always out dancing. You don't mind being alone

with me, do you?"

"I'm not sure yet."

He folded his hands in front of him and studied her face. In time, his mind's finger was tracing the sharp line of her cheek, running up the side to pause on her temple and brush under her hair; then it swept up to her forehead, where it rested briefly, to move again down the gentle slope of her nose to her red lips, where it paused and felt her downward jet of breath, the lips which opened, and then the finger moved over her chin and under it to a little hollow, where it pressed upward and tilted back the face . . .

"Tell me, Miss Lee—" he began.

"Amber," she insisted, holding the eyes that touched her so.

"Tell me, Amber," he began again, "would you concur that an economy is committing suicide in which the purchase and sale of government securities are given far better tax treatment than investments in genuinely productive private issues?"

"What an odd question to ask now."

"It's as dry a question I can ask at this moment."

She looked at him with the first melancholy expression he'd seen on her. "Yes," she answered at last. "I agree that honorable men like you are being squeezed out of life."

He was barely able to contain the harshness in his voice. "Why do you say 'honorable'?"

She shook her head slowly, wisely, and answered, almost in a whisper, "A dishonorable man would never have put it that way, or have even ever bothered himself with the question. I believe it must hurt to be so called. But only for a while."

Her glance rose and became fixed on the pulsing vein on his forehead. He said, coveting the look in her eyes, "I've always admired the role of honor in Chinese culture."

And her eyes came down, and he saw the immediate reply in them: *Then don't fight it!* His desire to see those eyes closed with the pain he could cause in her, to take her face into his hands, to do things with her, to pay her back in her own coin—it all surged up from within him, because, as she had said that with her eyes, she reached forward and laid a cool hand over one of his.

He saw that she knew she was in danger, and he saw her eyes drink it in. She would not remove her hand; he enjoyed having it there with the torture of not moving his in response. There was a fearful kind of pleasure in her eyes, something he recognized in himself. "Evidence to the contrary," he said, "but you don't chase men, do you?"

"I had no reason to develop the necessary technique, until now."

"Your men can't be won by technique. Not in any sense that counts."

"Neither can your women."

"You'll be joining a very exclusive club then," smiled Fury. "Do you think you can afford the dues?"

"To take you at face value, the way you want—yes, I can afford that."

"You're very good at it," he said.

She whispered, "And you."

He committed himself to the reality of her and to what he was feeling, and, allowing the wonder of it to work its way on him, turned his hand over and grasped hers firmly. She moved her head slightly in response to it, and her eyes flashed amber once before the lashes closed serenely over them.

I'm going to have this woman, he thought. If it's the last thing I do, I'm going to have her. I owe it to myself.

✻   ✻   ✻   ✻   ✻

"One of you is *very* fast."

They looked up and both withdrew their hands. Annette Hitchings stood above them with a pleased, mischievous grin.

"But I'm not certain who." Speake came up behind her and held her chair, and sat down and asked Amber with a wink, "Well, child, have you wrung the truth out of him? And I was just telling Merritt how good I am at pairing people."

"Yes," replied Amber, crossing her legs and leaning back to look at Fury. "I have the truth now. He's a bastard, the son of several fathers—all renegades and incorruptible outcasts—and of one of the happiest women in the world. He takes neither a yes nor a no for an answer, because he never bothers to ask. One day the world will look at him wrong, and he will slap its face."

Her answer caused even the worldly Miss Hitchings to blush. After momentary speechlessness, she shook her head in amused incomprehension. "Er, dear, I think you have your words confused. Don't you mean 'incorrigible'?"

Amber narrowed her eyes. Fury saw an added element of certainty in them which could not have come from their moments alone. "That, too," she said.

Speake signalled their waiter, then turned to Fury. "Is this true, Merritt? Are you our new scourge of the earth?"

Fury forgot what his reply had been. What remained of the evening became sweet agony; he'd never been at a loss for words before and he found it difficult to follow the conversation. They had two coffees and one brandy toast more. At last he was outside again, enjoying a cool breeze in his face, waiting for the attendants to bring the cars around.

"I have a full house tomorrow besides seeing Harry to collect my check and settle matters, Merritt," said Speake. "And tomorrow night I'm off to Sydney again to see about a ton of ocelot pelts that should have flown in from Brazil yesterday, so I shan't see you again until next week. Why don't we talk up a new company, something along the lines of Bluelist? I'm sure we could interest Bernardo and perhaps Jumpei, too."

"Good idea," said Fury. "I've already given it some thought.

Bluelist doesn't have the chocolates yet."

"And a word of caution, lad," said Speake, taking his hand. "Don't aggravate Harry. I can't elaborate on that because I don't understand yet what I feel. I like Harry, but something about him has reared its ugly head, and on no account can it be sex."

"I'll be careful not to upset him any more than is necessary," said Fury.

"Right. Well," said the Australian, looking at Miss Hitchings, "Annette and I are going to do a few clubs." He kissed Amber affectionately on the cheek, and Fury accepted a forceful peck on the mouth from Miss Hitchings.

"Don't forget our luncheon, Merritt," she said.

Amber answered before Fury could reply. "I rather think Mr. Fury will have dinner on his mind from now on, Annette," she purred, winding an arm around one of his possessively.

Speake led Miss Hitchings away before she could recover, and waved a last time to Fury.

When they were in his MGB, Amber said, as he started the motor, "I don't want to go home so early, but you must have business to do tomorrow, and you must be tired."

"I've nothing scheduled until noon," said Fury. "And I'm not tired. My pleasure is at your disposal."

"I can show you a view of Hong Kong few tourists have ever seen."

"Where?"

"My home."

Fury drove back along Nathan. Amber sat close to her door, at an angle, and watched him drive, and asked him questions. "What do you specialize in—besides anything?"

"Calculators, stationery, radios, ladies' lingerie—just about everything."

"You can't be satisfied with that. What do you really want?"

He told her about his plans to start his own investment bank in Switzerland, and how he would use it to take over companies he thought were being run the wrong way. When he was finished, he glanced over at her. Her expression was hidden in shadow. He looked back to the traffic. "But all that and the bank are years off. I wouldn't attempt it unless I had a lot of capital to throw around. I want to do it right the first time."

"As usual," spoke the shadow.

"As usual," grinned Fury. "If this trip is half as successful as I expect, I'll be able to start planning my bank within three years."

Amber said nothing for a while. He glanced over at her again. Her face was still in shadow, a cross wind blowing her hair. He turned his attention back to his driving.

She asked, as they came out of the Tunnel, "How can you make money when the odds are against you?"

"The gods smile upon me. Remember?"

"Only," she said cautiously, "if you are a criminal."

He chuckled. There was that urgent telegram again. No doubt about it. And if that was the case, there was no point in denying it. He said, "My propensity for breaking laws is surpassed only by some people's proclivity for making them."

"Would you break Hong Kong law?"

"I haven't found that necessary yet."

Amber reached into her purse and lit them both a cigarette from the dashboard lighter, then curled her legs comfortably under her and leaned her head on the head rest so she could watch him. "What do you do when you're not breaking laws or selling ladies' lingerie?"

"Read," he replied. "Quite a lot of reading. And box. Shoot. Dabble in the martial arts."

"Shoot?"

"Yes. Small arms, mostly handguns. I practice on a friend's farm in upstate New York."

"Are you good?"

"Good enough to be dangerous to what I'm aiming at."

"And why do you box, and 'dabble' in martial arts?"

"It keeps me fit. It also gives me the break I need from business, clears my mind, sharpens it." He paused. "And—I don't feel as vulnerable as I suppose I should be."

"Vulnerable? To what?"

"To the way things have been going. Not that I think my being able to shoot or flatten someone's nose or chop off his head will do me any good in the long run, but knowing how has come in handy in the short-term. Then there are all the stale Munchkin Lands people are opting for lately, with all their flower-decked appeals not to smoke, not to use sugar, not to pollute, not to waste energy, to be nice and always brake for animals and smile, smile, smile." Fury grunted in disgust as he remembered what he had left behind in New York. "I'm not a Class A candidate for residency in anyone's utopia. No psychoanalyst would make much money off my problems; I'd admit alienation from the word go and let *him* worry about it."

Amber moved closer to him and dressed a hand on his shoulder. He felt her studying his profile intently. She asked, "Have you ever killed?"

Fury frowned. "That's an odd question to ask a businessman."

"I can't imagine your coming this far—as you are—without having to have killed someone."

The muscles in his neck stiffened. As though in answer he felt her cool fingertips stroke one of the tendons. He turned to her, and saw a look of knowledge in her eyes. "It isn't that fascinating a subject with me," he said. "Is it with you?"

When she didn't answer immediately, Fury turned his attention back to the road.

"No," Amber replied after a moment. "It's just that I can't imagine your living without that possibility. You're an endangered species. You can't be blind to that. You must be your own protector. There are gangs of hoodlums in Hong Kong who would kill or maim without the slightest chance of gain. You're in danger from them and also from nice, respectable people who sit around polished committee tables and pledge allegiance to flags and write laws. One day they are going to want to corner you and destroy you, just so they can see you wishing you were really dead."

No, he wasn't blind to it. "I have my options, Amber. Don't think I won't exercise them—or never have." Fury looked at her. "Does that answer your question?"

"I knew the answer. I wanted to hear it from you." She leaned closer to him and shook her head so that her hair brushed his face for one brief, tantalizing second. His reaction to it was instant, but she pressed her fingers to his cheek and kissed his ear with lips that whispered, "Don't ever change." Then, just as suddenly, she moved away with a slow, deliberate rasp of her nylons, watching all the while how the sound affected him.

He rewarded her with an honest sigh. "Scheming lynx," he chuckled.

"Are you like this all the time?" she asked.

"How am I?"

"Strong. Happy. Tense."

"I suppose," he shrugged. "I never notice." He looked at her. "Are you like *that* all the time?" He took a last drag on the cigarette and flicked it out the window.

"When it suits me."

She lived near the top of one of the tall, slim, round towers that were poised like so many assorted colored pencils on the sides of Victoria Peak, overlooking the Central District and the harbor from recessed elevations. Her only window was a curving sheet of glass that was a wall of her living room. Fury looked out at the lights below. It was dark in the apartment;

Amber said it was the only way to enjoy the view at this time of night. "When the monsoon season begins, you can see the storms coming long before they arrive, walls of black and brown clouds holding powerful winds and billions of drops of rain. And you look down there at the tiny buildings and ships and lights and you think it's all too fragile to survive the sky when it falls on us. And the wind and rain and lightning descend, and do their worst, and when they are gone, we remain."

He turned to her. She was still in the middle of the room, where he'd left her. She had taken off her ascot and blazer, and stood watching him, her hands behind her back. "Come here," she smiled. "I have something to show you."

As he moved toward her, she brought her arms around and slowly undid her blouse, holding his eyes all the while. When he was near her, the blouse slid off her shoulders and fell to drape from her elbows. She thrust her breasts forward, straining her shoulders back, then lightly cupped her hands under them in an unmistakable gesture of offering.

He gripped her shoulders. In the last moments of that particular consciousness, he felt the band in his mind melt and dissolve and add to the heat of a new awareness. He jerked her to him and kissed her on answering lips and they both fought for air.

世界盡頭的光

Chapter 6

Facing
the
Gorgon

Eons later, he opened his eyes when he felt her hair brushing over his face. "It's seven, love," she said, "and I must be going."

He lay there, watching her dress and prepare for work. She put on a gray business suit. At one point she smoothed her skirt down needlessly, her palms stopping on her tilted front thighs. Her eyes sparkled at him, and she said in soft triumph, "Tired?"

"Weightless," he smiled.

She flashed him a proud, shameless grin and reached for her shoulder bag. "Tonight?"

"Seven?"

She nodded. "I'll wear what I should have worn last night."

"Shall I meet you here?"

"No. I'll pick *you* up. At your hotel."

"Fine," he laughed.

"I may have something special to show you."

Nothing that I can't know already, said his eyes.

"Good day." She bent down and gave him a kiss designed to provoke memories, then broke away before he could hold her and strode briskly out of the bedroom and disappeared through the sunshine pouring in through her living room window beyond.

*   *   *   *   *

He thought the name should have been given to some notoriously treacherous channel or stretch of shoreline near Hong Kong, but there was the Gorgon's Head restaurant, an otherwise anonymous, low-slung yellow brick building in the Sai Ying Pun "ladder street" bazaar near the Central District, with a set of thick bronze doors with intricately carved claws, and tiny round porthole windows set high off the pavement, wedged in between two six-story buildings, from which hung a myriad of exclusively Chinese character signs.

Guarding the doors and the little alcove was an enormous granite Gorgon's head with a wide Oriental face. It was about three feet tall, ten feet around, and sat on a pedestal of green marble that had a red dot on each of its corners. It stared back at Fury with blood-shot eyes in a pained, malevolent expression, done in various hues of green, with faded touches of pink in the cheeks and around the mouth and eyes, which were yellow. The mouth, a glistening red oval, was frozen in the pronunciation of some silent warning. The writhing, snapping snakes—about thirty of them—that made up the creature's scalp were of an especially revolting shade of green with a wet patina gloss. They, too, had yellow eyes, and red, flicking tongues.

But something was missing, he realized after a moment—the thing had no teeth. He also noticed that there was no name above the entrance, nor a street number, only a modest plastic plate on a wall near the doors bearing the little red sampan of the Hong Kong Tourist Association. The bust was probably identification enough.

I hope it isn't a reflection on the food, he remarked to himself as he passed the head and went inside.

He should have expected what he saw inside: Next to nothing, not counting the moving spots of luminescence which were scantily clad Chinese waitresses whose faces and gloves were done in glow paint. Something that was not quite music hung in the darkness, delicate, random, metallic notes which followed one another in no discernible pattern or rhythm. Fury expected to trip on something at any moment as he followed the hostess to where Briscoe sat. It was a booth far in the rear, lit by a dim overhead Chinese lamp. He could see only vague shapes of other guests and tables under other lamps, and hear an undertone of babbling voices which seemed to come from another room, except that there was no other room.

Briscoe stood up and offered his hand. Fury shook it as heartily as he could; there was no point in telegraphing his intentions. When they sat down, Fury said, "You have an atrocious taste in restaurants, Harry. I must remember never to recommend this place."

"You haven't tried the cuisine yet, Merritt," replied Briscoe, snapping his serviette open and spreading it on his lap. "Don't judge a restaurant by its hallucinations."

The lack of lighting did nothing to enhance Briscoe's face. His deeply recessed eyes were only bright pins of white light lost somewhere over the width of his cheeks, like two campfires on the edge of a distant cliff. "Well, I only hope the kitchen is better lighted," said Fury. "Do they have a specialty?" He spread his own serviette and poured himself a tumbler of warm wine from the bottle Briscoe had already opened, and tasted it. It lingered very briefly on his tongue, then was gone.

"This is a *dim sum* place," said Briscoe. "The ladies you barely see will come by with trays and tell you what they have on them, and you take your pick." He smiled at Fury's frown.

"And don't belittle the wine. It's specially made and not meant to be anything more than an alternative wash-down to tea. Or would you prefer tea?" he asked, reaching for a fat blue porcelain pot. Fury nodded. Briscoe poured him a cup, then one for himself. "Oh," he added, "See won't be joining us right away. Something came up at one of his banks. I forget what and which."

Fury hunted in vain for the pins of light, but they were bent over the teacup. So Pok *was* coming. He decided not to pursue the matter, and sampled the tea. It was better, but definitely not a substitute for a good wine. And the tea made him aware that the wine had left a taste in his mouth, one close to rancid butter.

Briscoe said, with no difficulty Fury could sense, "I . . . want to apologize for my . . . words to you yesterday. I become very hot under the collar when things don't go my way. I'm a natural tantrum thrower and you wouldn't believe some of the foolish things I've said to people in the past. If it makes you feel any better, you should know that I've mouthed my way out of quite a few lucrative contracts."

Fury managed his best dead-pan and replied, "No apology needed. I don't take offense at people's occasional slips of tongue. I knew you couldn't mean what you said. I'd forgotten it half an hour later."

"A very cool character you are, Merritt," smiled Briscoe. He took another sip of tea. "Oh, did you notice the statue outside?"

Fury grinned. "I think it noticed me."

Briscoe chuckled. "Frightening troll, isn't it?"

Fury shrugged. "If one takes those things seriously."

"One should take some things seriously. Did you happen to notice the red dots on the base?"

Just then a waitress materialized at their table. The girl recited a short list of what was in the bowls of her tray. It was eerie and unsettling to watch her glowing face move. The paint must do wonders for her complexion, thought Fury. Briscoe chose a bowl of golf-ball sized dumplings, and Fury a bowl of buttered steak puffs. "The red dots?" he said, forking a puff into his mouth. "Yes, I noticed them." The puff almost melted before he could begin to chew it.

"You know what they signify?"

"No."

"They're the mark of a triad."

Fury saw what was coming—another protection racket. He decided not to appear so ignorant of the local "culture." "I wasn't aware that criminal organizations gave restaurant ratings."

Briscoe shook his head, amused. "No, not a bit of it. Those dots mean that this establishment has an insurance policy with that 'criminal organization.'"

"Don't you mean a 'protection' policy? 'We protect you from harm for a price or we harm you for free.'"

Briscoe forked a dumpling into his mouth. "Used to mean that. But that's all antiquity now. The 'Dying Stars'—the four dots are their mark—used to be one of the most powerful and feared triads in these parts years and years ago. No longer, though. All the triads have declined. But there are still some places left that hire a triad's chop, mostly out of tradition and for tourist value."

Another steak-puff melted in Fury's mouth, and he took a sip of tea. "Yes," he said, "I imagine there's much more to be made smuggling gold or Red Chinese poppy products than in extortion anyway." He glanced at Briscoe as he said it. Briscoe had been busy with the dumplings, but paused imperceptibly while forking one into his open mouth.

"There's a write-up on triads on the menu here," said Briscoe, one side of his mouth full. "Positively gory. They only put it on for the tourists. Gives them a thrill, I suppose."

Fury glanced around. "What menu?"

Briscoe looked at him, his fork poised with another dumpling. "The one they hand you if you don't know what the hell you're doing here." He stuck the dumpling in, then reached for his wine tumbler to wash it down. "That one was a bit too salty."

Fury felt that Briscoe was trying to tell him something. He didn't think the man had changed much in attitude since yesterday and had invited him here for a buttering up he perhaps just wasn't delicate enough to pull off. Rancid butter, mused Fury—just like that wine.

The waitress came again with another tray. Fury selected a bowl of what looked like miniature hot-cross buns.

Briscoe was still busy with the dumplings. Fury wondered if he was waiting for Pok to arrive to launch into the subject of Bluelist. That was fine with him. Pok's reaction would be just as interesting as Briscoe's. He tried one of the buns. It dissolved like sugar on his tongue before he had a chance to bite into it. He frowned; nothing had substance here. "How's lumber?" he asked, just to fill the silence.

Briscoe took a breather from the dumplings. "Very steady at the moment. But there'll be a big pickup in demand in a few months. Couple of syndicates are going to build up the west side and Wanchai. New commercial complex on the boards for Nathan Road, too. I'm set for the next few years here. And Singapore's wondering whether to build a subway or a monorail system. Either way they'll need plenty of lumber. Haven't asked for bids yet, but I have my word in with every major contractor from here to San Francisco." Briscoe paused. "You?"

Fury decided to risk it. He sipped some tea, then said, "Fine. All things considered, I called in the chocolate order. It'll be here in a week."

Briscoe's fork stopped in mid-air. "Well," he said tentatively, "you really shouldn't have, Merritt." He paused. "You *have* seen Derek since the meeting, haven't you?"

"Yes," said Fury, studying a bun before he ate it. "I thought he'd have stayed in after all—but we'll talk when See comes. Right?"

Briscoe was obviously taken off-stride. He chose a bowl of steak-puffs this time, and ate with less enthusiasm and at a much slower pace. Twice he glanced at his watch. Finally he thumped his fork down. "I *don't* understand you, Merritt!" he exclaimed. "Yesterday you practically thumb your nose at us. Now you're taking up the cause! Why?"

Fury shrugged. "You'll like those puffs, Harry. Can't imagine how they do it."

"Why did you change your mind??" insisted Briscoe.

Fury smiled innocently. "Why? Well, I always rely on my own judgment, Harry. Last night I asked myself, 'What *do* I know?' So I made an exception to my rule. If you're so confident in an expansion project, why shouldn't I be?"

Briscoe stared at him, unable to answer that. He took a gulp of his tea, not taking his eyes off of Fury. He said, "That doesn't sound plausible, coming from *you*, Merritt! You're so damned independent you're . . . you're like a separate country! You ought to knit your own flag!" He leaned an inch closer. "What are you up to?"

Fury only had time to smile broadly when Pok appeared out of the darkness. He shook Fury's hand, did not look at Briscoe, but slid into the booth beside him. Pok was all smiles. "I beg your pardon for my tardiness," he said with the rush of an actor trying to catch up on his cues. "I was detained by un-expected problems." A cup and saucer appeared before him, and a fresh pot of tea. Briscoe, composing himself with effort, poured him a cup in deference. "How is the lunch?" asked Pok, nodding acknowledgement to Briscoe, but addressing Fury. "I hope my culinary artists have pleased you."

"Your artists, Mr. Pok?" asked Fury.

"Why, yes!" answered Pok proudly. "Did not Harry tell you? One of my first and finest investments many years ago. I do not own very many restaurants, but the ones I do make money. The Gorgon's Head is almost as much an institution in Hong Kong as the Star Ferry and the noon-day gun. It makes money, no?"

"I can't say," smiled Fury. "I imagine it would be difficult counting anything here. Especially your customers."

Pok laughed. "It has become famous as a rendezvous for secret lovers who wish to dine in privacy and—"

Briscoe cut him short with a terse statement in Chinese. Pok abruptly frowned. He glanced at Fury once, then averted his eyes. A waitress came, and bowed to him without tipping a bowl or plate on her tray. She recited in Chinese what she had. He took some time to make up his mind, seeming to be too distracted to study the dishes. Finally he chose some brownish cakes and a bowl of fish soaked with an odd, bluish sauce.

Fury sat quietly, listening to the soft jarring notes that came from nowhere. His eyes had become adjusted and he could see little blurs of light around the room. The waitresses, bright, shimmering oscillations, moved about constantly, softly calling out their wares like subdued cigarette girls. They reminded him of a pool of fish. In fact, the whole setting here had the distinct aura of dining deep in an underwater grotto. He supposed that he should feel cornered and alone here, much more susceptible to pressure from Pok and Briscoe.

Neither of them said anything for a while. Pok concentrated on his fish and cakes, and Briscoe on his steak-puffs. Fury lit a cigarette, waited, and watched.

Pok finally looked up with a weak smile. "Mr. Briscoe says you are keen to remain in the company, Merritt. Why so?"

Pok had never addressed him by his first name before. It had always been a very formal "Mr. Fury." He grasped for the first time the gulf that existed between himself and these men. He thought he had been closer to Briscoe, and now realized that his "Merritt" had been a condescension. Pok thought him a child. Fury answered him amiably, "I explained to Harry that I was wrong to doubt his judgment in the matter of expanded tungsten production. In which case I see no reason to leave such a . . . windfall . . . to you two gentlemen alone."

Pok stared at him. There wasn't much he could say, either.

Briscoe spoke. "Look, Merritt," he smiled, "don't go by what *I* say. *I* may very well be wrong after all. If you stay on, it will still mean you and See and I will need to commit ourselves to a lot of money. You'll probably tie up your credit and capital here and in the States for three or more years." He shook his head. "I don't think you're ready, frankly speaking. Just not yet, that is. Say that we *are* wrong about this expansion. See and I are in much better positions to absorb any losses. You aren't, Merritt. I know that for a fact. You'd be wiped off the board. You'd probably need to take a management position somewhere and be obliged to take orders and scrimp by on a salary. You don't strike me as corporate zombie material, Merritt. In fact—in very blunt point of fact—I doubt if anyone would have you by today's corporate standards. You're just not one to mouth service to society or humanity or any other bung-ho line of utilitarian foolishness they all plead these times. Service to yourself, that's your motto, Merritt. And mine, and See's. But that's the background, like it or not. I simply don't advise your staying on." Briscoe paused. "Do you see my reasoning?"

"I see it," said Fury. "And I couldn't agree with you more."

"So," continued Briscoe, jauntily popping one of the steak-puffs into his mouth, "we're prepared to make you a much better offer than we did the others. How does—*three times* your original interest strike you?"

"Exorbitant," smiled Fury. "Probably four times what the mine is worth. What did you offer Walter?"

Pok's glasses darted back to his food. Briscoe said, "There you go again!" He studied Fury for a moment, then screwed his face up. "If you're so blasted sure the mine is worthless, why are you so determined to stay on??"

"Sheer curiosity," replied Fury. "I can't help but wonder why you would want to keep it all to yourselves."

Briscoe planted an elbow on the table top and used his fork as a pointer. He wagged it sharply several times, his mouth open, about to say something, but he gave up the effort and settled for stabbing at one of the steak-puffs, disintegrating it.

Pok studied Fury over the rim of his teacup. He put it down, then folded his hands gracefully. "There is an old Chinese proverb, Mr. Fury," he smiled. "A strong reed bends with the wind."

Fury barely suppressed a laugh. "Pardon me, Mr. Pok, but I think your old proverb is about twenty seconds young."

Pok replied angrily, "Even so! It is a proverb that would be harkened by wise men!"

Fury smiled and captured the old man's eyes. "It would seem that some reeds break and are blown into the water."

"Please?"

"Your predecessor at Felicity Bank—a Mr. Chan Ha Tze, if I recall correctly—was found floating in the harbor not too long ago. Did he recommend lowering the prime rate?"

Pok frowned and glanced once at a glaring Briscoe, then his features smoothed and he said, "Mr. Ha Tze's death was most unfortunate and regrettable." He hesitated. "We do not know why he died. Possibly he was under the influence of extortionists. Such things are not uncommon here, Mr. Fury."

"You win the understatement award of the year, Mr. Pok. What could a respectable banker have in common with a frustrated union tycoon, such as Kwong Lai, except a watery funeral?"

Pok stiffened. Briscoe's stare remained unchanged. Pok said,

"I do not know this other person. I do not share the Western fascination for lurid crime stories."

"But apparently you risk the same fate," said Fury. "It's an awfully severe form of sacking. I'm not sure I'd want to work in your bank, or even take a loan from it."

Pok's lips pursed, and his eyes grew hard.

Fury continued. "But—you must have come highly recommended to the Houghton-Devane Group." As he said it, he glanced briefly at Briscoe; the skin around the man's temples twitched at the sound of the name. "What I don't understand, though, is what kind of bank Felicity could be that it would put several million dollars behind a ghost of a chance. You certainly didn't rise from refugee rags to riches that way, Mr. Pok." He paused. "Or were they just stage rags?"

"Restrain your certainty," replied Pok ominously. "You are discussing things of which you are ignorant. Woefully ignorant."

Briscoe broke in with sarcastic bravado. "What next, Fury?? The bloody communists?? See, are there Red Guards lurking in your cash box? Mr. Fury here is concerned!"

Pok turned ashen. "I would not know. Money does not parade the identity of its owners."

"How convenient," remarked Fury.

Briscoe virtually bared his teeth at him. "The next thing we know he'll be waving a bloody American flag!" He poured himself a tea with distracted, shaking hands.

Fury reached over and took the pot from him. As he refilled his own cup, he said, with too casual diffidence, "Long may it wave over such as me."

Briscoe almost choked on the tea he was sipping. He wiped his mouth with the serviette, then threw it down. "As antiquated a sentiment as I've ever heard, Fury! In fact, I'm not at all sure I've *ever* heard it! But don't worry, my friend! It'll wave, for sure, but over your blasted grave—if anyone cares to tend it!" He nudged Pok in the ribs and nodded to Fury. "Mr. *Tu Li,*" he scoffed, "alias Patrick Henry, See. It's a joke, but wasn't I right about him? Didn't I tell you?"

Pok merely pouted in apparent confirmation.

Fury stirred his cup. "Your mind seems fixed on flags today, Harry."

Briscoe stared at him defiantly.

Fury said, "You know something? Neither of you ever asked me why I chose chocolates for the tax scheme."

Briscoe repeated his sarcasm. "Please *do* let us in on your ingenious strategy!"

Fury faced Pok instead. "It's the least likely import to be re-exported to Red China."

"How foresighted of you," jeered Briscoe. "And for your information, it's referred to here as the People's Republic of China."

Fury assumed a thoughtful attitude. "First of all, Harry— for your information—it's not a 'republic' but a dictatorship; of or for whom is strictly academic. Further, if a man who had schizophrenic paranoidal tendencies complicated by persecution fantasies committed murder, would one call him a schizophrenic paranoidal persecution fantasizer, or a murderer?" He paused. "*Red* China, Harry. It's more economical and Peking's favorite color to boot. It shouldn't mind it a bit. After all, red figures greatly in its flags, silk and purges."

"You *are* the puritan, Fury," said Briscoe with quiet, fixed finality. "Perhaps you'd better leave. But you have been such an entertaining, *interesting* guest."

Fury looked at Pok. "Do you wish me to leave, Mr. Pok?"

The man looked down into his bowl and replied in a raspy voice, "Most earnestly, Mr. Fury."

Fury rose, bowed slightly, and said, "Thank you, gentlemen, for the lunch. However, the time invested by us at this table has been much more productive than that mine will ever be."

Briscoe stared back up at him. "Don't pursue it, Fury," he said, wagging the fork again. "Just don't trouble yourself. I mean *that*—sincerely."

✿   ✿   ✿   ✿   ✿

Mission accomplished, thought Fury as he slid into the MGB, which he'd parked a few blocks away from the restaurant. Their move next. Briscoe and Pok wanted no one else in on their tungsten scheme, and especially not himself, not now. Options open to them? Very few; two at the most. They could take him into their confidence and proceed as announced.

Or they could kill him—and proceed as announced.

Fury reached into the dashboard for his sunglasses, then turned the motor to life and pulled out into the traffic, headed for the Cross Harbour Tunnel. It was a lovely blue, warm day for a drive through the New Territories. About an hour's drive. He needed a place to think. Bluelist Mine at the foot of Cloudy Hill was the right place for it.

Once he was through Lion Rock Tunnel in New Kowloon the pace became less pressing. The surroundings abruptly changed from the visible and audible ruckus of the city to the quiet silence of the countryside. There were more mountains and gently rolling green hills, little patches of pine and leafed trees in an otherwise treeless landscape, and far fewer people. He passed farms and rice paddies, and once honked his horn in warning at a high school bicycle picnic strung out along the two-lane road. The students cheered the sight of his MGB as it raced past them. The road hugged the meandering Tolo Bay shoreline and skirted the mountains to his left. Just beyond the oddly placed Chinese University even this thinned out and he was in virtually uninhabited parts. The hills became larger without losing their charm and the concrete pavement gave way to dirt and crushed rock.

Cloudy Hill was about three miles from Starling Inlet to the east and three from the border with Red China to the north. Bluelist was dug into the foot of the hill, consisting of one shaft entrance, some out-buildings, and the unused ore processing plant about thirty yards from the shaft entrance. A wire fence—erected at the behest of the Colonial government to deny refugees from across the border a place to hide—enclosed the property, and the place only saw human activity three days a week, when Ushio's mineworkers were bussed in from granite quarries from far across the Territories. There was no watchman; the gates were locked after the work crews left.

They were locked now. Fury drove by and followed the road around the next hill. He got out, took off his jacket, and climbed the grassy slope to the top. From here he could see the entire property. He sat down, lit a cigarette, and thought about the mine below, trying to make sense of the pieces of the puzzle.

Bluelist Number Four had once been the exclusive property of the Shota Trading Company—Ushio's company—and Ushio had been on the verge of re-opening it when he was approached by Briscoe about a year and a half ago. The mine was last worked twenty years before and had since collapsed. The shorings had rotted and given way, and the shaft was flooded. It was Briscoe's idea to share half the re-opening costs, to redirect all the tungsten income—minus the profits, which were to be Ushio's—back into the Bluelist common fund. By agreement, Shota Trading could do what it liked with anything else that came out of the mine.

Bluelist Number Four was a lode mine, basically a cassiterite lode, something very rare in these parts, a geological exception to the rule. There was, of course, tungsten, but not in sufficient or pure enough amounts to justify the working of the mine. Ushio made his money on the cassiterite—or tin—which was present in the ore four to five times over the tungsten. He stockpiled the ore in the sheds until he had enough to justify having one or two trucks come out to the mine to haul it to New Kowloon and a freighter. The freighter then took it to Japan and Shota's processing plants.

It had also been Briscoe's idea to build the processing plant. But when the first ore came out a single test of it made them realize that it would be foolhardy to construct a plant here just for tungsten. Harry still insisted that one be built. Shota would not agree to even split the construction costs. The partnership seemed on the verge of splitting up when Briscoe had yet another idea: Bluelist Tungsten Trading. That was where the rest of the partners came in. Harry introduced See first—who insisted on spreading the risk further—then Derek Speake, Pelosi, Ronquillo, and finally Fury. Thus was raised the one hundred thousand dollars to build a basic gravity separator for tungsten.

And there it stood below, a white elephant.

Fury recalled what he had been thinking the evening before and was reluctant to tell Derek. The States produced tungsten, but practically no tin. Briscoe simply wasn't interested in the tin. It was the tungsten he was after, thought Fury. Ushio had told him, in a private conversation during his first visit to Hong Kong a year ago, that Red China had the biggest tungsten deposits in the world, seven or eight times those of the States. But the Mainland was pitifully backward in mining technology. What tungsten it produced went mainly to Britain and Sweden. As high as American labor costs were, though, Chinese tungsten simply could not compete with other producers, even though Peking had plenty of cheap labor to mine it.

What he had wanted to tell Derek was that slave labor was never a profitable proposition—not unless one had a monopoly on what slaves produced. He did not half believe the idea last night; now he was certain of it.

He heard the sound of tires rolling over gravel and looked down at the mine. Three cars had pulled up in a line at the gates: Jumpei's Datsun, a gray Rolls limousine and a Mercedes limousine. Jumpei went to the gates and unlocked them, then returned to his car and led the procession into the compound, stopping in front of the shack that served as an office. To his mild surprise, Fury saw Harry Briscoe get out of the Rolls with a tall, lanky man in a beige suit. The driver of the Mercedes rushed to open the door of the Mercedes for two more visitors, one of whom was See Pok. Fury recognized the fourth man, but had to think back before he could remember the name. When he remembered it, he smiled, because the puzzle was almost complete now. Fury rose and went back to his MGB.

They were all in the shack when he pulled up in front of it. He sat and let the motor idle. Briscoe came out first, then Ushio, followed by the others. Briscoe's jaw dropped. "What are *you* doing here?" he demanded.

"Hello, Harry. We can't see enough of each other," said Fury. He nodded to Ushio, who looked bewildered, and at Pok, who looked angry. Turning back to Briscoe, he said, "I was about to ask *you* the same thing."

Briscoe recovered quickly. "Well, why didn't you tell me you were coming out here, Merritt? We could have come together." Pok's traveling partner from the Mercedes came out of the shack then. "Err, let me introduce you to Mr. Rutledge, an engineer from London who's here to look over the property and draw up preliminary plans for the, err, expansion,"—Fury exchanged nods with the tall, lanky man—"and to Mr. Pan Chao, who is a colleague of See's at Felicity Bank. Gentlemen, this is Mr. Merritt Fury, a partner in Bluelist." Fury nodded cordially to the Chinese introduced as Mr. Chao; Mr. Chao did not return the acknowledgement.

Fury turned to Rutledge. "What firm are you with,

Mr. Rutledge?"

"Matheson and Tuttle," answered Rutledge in a bright, brisk voice. "Know us?"

"Yes. Wasn't it your firm that supervised the construction of the Ziba port facility for Saudi Arabia on the Red Sea? I understand that your colleagues in Jordan were harassed because now Ziba will threaten Aqaba's eminence as a primary port. How did you resolve the problem?"

Rutledge laughed. "Easily enough! We built the Jordanians a brand new airport complete with cargo handling facilities. Whatever good that'll do anyone there!"

"Very interesting," said Fury. "With so much work to be had from fools, what could bring you to this pitiful little mine? It can't be worth your attention."

"Don't you know?" began Rutledge. "We're here to—"

"—Pick out the best spot for the new buildings," cut in Briscoe abruptly. "You know—left or right of the plant here, see if it's feasible to pump water from the inlet. That sort of thing."

"You'll need a subcontractor to work all that out, Harry," piped Rutledge good-humoredly. "Not our line of work at all. We're strictly trans—"

Again Briscoe cut him off. "And Mr. Chao here—he wants to see everything. We plan to drive down to Tolo, too, and explore the feasibility of building our own dock facility for the ore."

Rutledge said, businesslike, "I've seen the maps, Harry, and we may have to dredge no matter what site we select—"

Pok interrupted him this time. "Mr. Chao is here to view the operation and get a better idea of a cost estimate."

Fury rested his hand on the stick shift. He looked up at Briscoe thoughtfully. "Harry, I've been such a fool."

Briscoe smirked, unable to disguise his pleasure. "If you insist, Merritt."

Fury shook his head. "You went shopping for fools and dupes when you put together Bluelist. But never say, 'It's all the same to me' when you find them, Harry. You just might be the same to your fool."

"I'll keep that in mind."

"Good day, gentlemen." Fury shifted into gear and got the hell out of there. Harry was a liar. So was Pok. Rutledge? Just the latest dupe. Ushio? He'd caught Ushio's confused, uncomprehending expression during the introductions. He didn't think the man was conscious of the game being played between any of the parties. But the silent Pan Chao was the biggest liar of them all.

Because his name wasn't Pan Chao; it was Lon Ping, Peking's observer without portfolio. Ping had refused to even smile when he was introduced. His eyes were frozen dead, beyond even malice. They were the eyes of a man who had already made a decision.

面對女怪戈耳工

Chapter 7

Dying Stars
and
Red Giants

The desk said there had been several calls for him from Tinto this afternoon; it was a little past four o'clock now. The phone was jangling in the bedroom when Fury walked into his suite. He took off his coat, threw it on the couch, and went to answer it, cursing himself for not having left a message for Tinto.

And he stopped cold in his tracks to face the two bellhops who were coming out, one of them carrying his briefcase. They both smiled, and one inquired, "Mr. Fury?"

Fury, more startled than confused, nodded acknowledgement, and impatiently made to pass the threshold to the phone, but stopped when the one carrying his briefcase deftly undid the snaps and pitched it back through the door. It crashed into the vanity table mirror and its contents exploded throughout the room with the broken glass.

When he looked at the bellhops again they were reaching into their brown, silk wrap-around jackets with their white gloves. "Please help us make this as painless as possible, Mr. Fury," said the other. "We bear you no personal grudge."

What they took out were knives, five-inch long, paper-thin

blades that curled inward at the tips to form hooks.

"I'll keep that in mind," replied Fury, edging back out into the drawing room. If they were going to attack him, he'd rather he had more room.

They understood, perhaps. When they thought he had moved far enough, they flanked his sides, holding their knives out front, waving them, wanting to rivet his attention on the gleaming, deadly blades. It was an effective means of mesmerizing a victim for an easy kill.

When he judged that he had gone far enough, Fury feigned a lunge at the one on his right, but whipped back to his left and met the other who had automatically closed his distance with a fist he slammed hard into the surprised face. He grabbed the wrist of the recoiling bellhop with both hands, pivoted slightly, brought up his knee, and broke the forearm, snatching the knife almost in mid-air as it dropped from the limping hand, leaving the bellhop to faint on his own as he turned to face the other.

The other had lost distance avoiding Fury's surprise lunge. Fury wondered why this one stayed now; the door was behind him, only five feet away, unlocked. If their purpose had been to kill him, there was little chance of that now.

But, no, he stood his ground, crouched down, weaving his torso back and forth in short, almost imperceptible movements, his knife low and ready to strike.

Fury took the initiative and moved slowly toward him, standing his full height. The phone continued to ring, and he realized that the bellhop was rocking in time to the phone's persistent queries.

Then it stopped. With a yell calculated to fill the abrupt silence the bellhop leaped and aimed for Fury's face. Fury dropped low, then sprung back up and grasped the bellhop's knife wrist while thrusting his own into the stomach, pushing him back and thudding him hard against the wall, twisting the blade as long as he felt resistance.

The bellhop's endurance was incredible. He was in too much pain to do much more with his free hand than clutch Fury's shirt at the shoulder for extra support, but he kept bucking off the wall and straining against the grip on his wrist. Fury gritted his teeth and pushed harder, touching bone with his knife, wondering how much more the boy could take. Finally, he forced the upheld arm down and bent it back on the corner of the bedroom door frame. He heard and felt bone snap at the same time the bellhop's knife thumped softly on the rug.

The body stopped straining, and Fury pushed himself away, his hands empty. The bellhop, his face squinched up in saintly pain, slid silently down the wall and collapsed.

The silence which followed the swiftness of the thing allowed his normal reaction to sink in. Fury stood for a moment, incredulous. They were simply two Chinese youths, probably in their teens, whom he might have picked out of a crowd of youths or from the regiment of bellhops who served the hotel. He stepped into the bedroom and saw the carnage for the first time: his clothes from the closet lay rumpled on the floor, and the drawers of the dresser had been taken out and emptied; the gun manuals, the business directory and the three Schiller volumes all had been pulled apart, the pages ripped to pieces and scattered over the room with his clothes.

Suddenly tired, Fury sat on the edge of the bed and stared with dazed amazement at the two boys. In time he noticed the blood on the wall and the gold pile rug, then on his right hand, tie, shirt and trousers. Involuntarily, he gulped. Only now did the blunt, heart-stopping awareness that comes with the near proximity of one's own death begin to numb his thoughts and actions. He hoisted himself up and went into the bathroom for a shower in freezing water.

Changed and refreshed, he poured himself a stiff drink at

the sidebar and took it back to the bedroom, where he sat on the bed again and used the phone. As he was speaking, he noticed the knife hand of the youth he had killed, still stretched out at the threshold of the bedroom door. When he was finished, he gently cradled the receiver and stooped down to inspect it. His grip on the boy's wrist must have slid up over the palm and peeled the white glove off as far as the fingertips. Tattooed on the knuckles were four red dots. Curious, he checked the knife hand of the unconscious youth.

Four red dots.

* * * * *

The police came, followed closely by the hotel manager. The police were efficient, the manager embarrassed. Nothing like this had ever happened before. Yes, there had been some trouble, he conceded; what hotel hadn't had any? But then it had been limited to drunken tiffs between men and their wives or mistresses. *Nothing* like this. We're very sorry and we'll lop a week off your bill, absolutely no charge for any of our services, either. Can't imagine where they got those uniforms from.

Before the men in white carted the body away, Inspector Hung of the Hong Kong Homicide Section, Central District, a trim, affable, articulate man in his late thirties, waved Fury over to it. He reached under the sheet and brought out a hand, the one with the red dots, and held it up as though it were a rare, exotic flower. "This is curious, is it not, Mr. Fury?"

"And painful," said Fury, looking at it. "It must have hurt like hell having those put on. Nothing but bone under skin."

"True," nodded Hung. "Do you know what they signify?"

Fury paused before answering. "A triad," he said. "The dots are its mark, its logo, so to speak. Having them put on was probably part of an initiation."

Inspector Hung smiled and replaced the hand, then nodded

to the men in white, who took the body out. "You are better acquainted with local 'color' than most foreign businessmen, Mr. Fury."

"I like to know something about the cities I do business in, Inspector."

Hung grunted dubious admiration. "I commend you on that, Mr. Fury. But there is more here than meets the eye. You were no mere victim of an interrupted burglary. I wish to discuss this with you. Please." He gestured to the chairs by the coffee table.

They sat. Hung instructed his uniformed men and the stenographer to wait for him outside. Then he leaned forward and folded his hands on a crossed knee. "Those red dots— they are the mark of the Dying Stars triad, Mr. Fury. Some old, dying stars turn into what astronomers call red giants, such as Antares and Betelgeuse, and perhaps even our own sun, some day. Others collapse into white dwarfs. You are familiar with astronomy, Mr. Fury?"

"Some. Not much."

"These triads—they usually don't cause serious trouble— not in this respect, at least. The triads were once powerful, but no longer. The intelligence agencies of many powers all attempted to use them at one time or another, but the triads proved to be too independent and unreliable. They were once societies of honor, but in time degenerated into mere criminal associations. Besides gold, narcotics and refugees, they have also been successful in contraband cigarettes and liquor. Very successful. American cigarettes and Japanese spirits are a major income source for them."

Fury smiled. "Lift your import duties on them, Inspector," he suggested. "Nothing encourages crime like prohibition and prohibitive taxes." He offered Hung one of his Rothmans; to his surprise, the officer accepted with a rueful smile. He took one himself and lit both of them.

"I am not unfamiliar with the billion dollar interstate cigarette smuggling business in your country, Mr. Fury," grinned Hung. "It is a topic well worth speculation."

"Most smugglers would agree. One would think that puritans were their best friends."

After a draught of smoke, Hung continued. "However— this topic. It is extremely odd that you would be the target of an attack. Acts of homicide are not common outside the bounds of these triads. And—these people are rarely found in our juvenile courts. They are youngsters in an adult organization one would not otherwise notice, junior members, usually, with no prestige or status." Hung paused to savor the Rothman again. "But—those knives—they are ceremonial knives, awarded to Dying Star members on their fifth year of membership, and to members of junior standing who have outstanding records of service to the society.

"Now, Mr. Fury: they can only have done this on order. Would you know why?"

Fury shook his head. "No, Inspector, I would not."

"There must be *some* reason," smiled Hung. "They don't attack tourists or foreign businessmen. They are not sneak thieves or petty felons."

"I'm sorry, Inspector, but I can't account for it."

Hung sat, silent with unshaken doubt.

Fury said, "I'm a genuine businessman, Inspector. I've spent, all told, perhaps two months in Hong Kong. I can refer you to several commercial people here, although I know that wouldn't necessarily prove anything. You've seen my passport; you may think it's bogus. Basically, you don't really know who I am. I'm in the habit of making true statements, but then you have no reason to accept my veracity, either. I know that you suspect me of other than open-and-shut innocence in this matter. Why?"

Hung's eyes seemed to appreciate Fury's frankness. "Businessmen," he began, "particularly Western businessmen, are a generally helpless lot. By rights *you* should have been found dead on the carpet over there, the Homicide Section should be in confusion over who could have possibly killed you, and the hotel management should be in hysterics as to how to keep it all quiet.

"But that is *not* the scenario. One apparently professional killer, somewhat expert with custom-made knives, is dead— very professionally dead! Another has had his arm broken, his left jaw dislocated, and will be in hospital for weeks—very professionally disabled! And his triad has sworn him to secrecy in all things; he will most likely attempt suicide before he reveals anything to us. And yourself? *You* emerge from close combat without a scratch!

"Can you not *now* see my dilemma, Mr. Fury? It is not a textbook problem: Given X, then Y. You are neither an X nor a Y. Your continued good health implies another problem altogether, one containing more than one unknown quantity. Why is that, Mr. Fury?"

Fury considered an answer other than the whole truth; for the moment, what truth he knew himself was his to pass along as he saw fit. He said, "I can tell you why one is dead and the other injured. It's because I'm an expert shot with hand-guns, I box a great deal, and I attend one of the finest martial arts schools in New York. I have engaged in these activities for years, first because they give me leisure, and then because I travel widely and there are many parts of the world in which I feel much safer knowing these things."

Hung merely notched his eyebrows in dissatisfaction.

Fury continued. "Now, though I agree with you that killing me was their only purpose, I simply don't know why that was their purpose. All I can say is that they went about it as a ritual. They were determined to kill, or die trying."

Hung wrinkled his brow in mock admiration. "So—you

can *kill*, Mr. Fury?"

"I can die, too, Inspector, but I'm in no rush to prove that, either."

Hung leaned forward in confidence. "Mr. Fury, I have been endeavoring to ask you if you have any enemies in Hong Kong. That is all."

"None that I'm aware of."

Hung said nothing for a long moment. He studied his cigarette, then said, "Kwong Lai."

Fury smiled to disguise his reaction. "I'm sorry," he said, "but my Chinese is practically nonexistent."

Hung chuckled. "Kwong Lai is a name. You do not recall hearing it ever before?"

"No."

"Then perhaps Chan Ha Tze?"

"Nor that."

Hung sighed and flicked his ashes into the tray. "So you are a businessman. Do you represent a company, or are you independent; that is, self-employed?"

"Both," said Fury. "I'm a partner in Bluelist Tungsten Trading, but I trade for my own account."

Hung frowned briefly, then his brow lightened again. "Ah, yes," he smiled. "Sir Harry Briscoe's enterprise, I believe. A fine man," he nodded. "And of course a fine business."

Fury nodded noncommittal agreement.

"How long have you been associated with him?"

"For just over a year. Since we formed the company."

"This is, I am sure, an extraneous, presumptuous question, Mr. Fury, so please forgive me for asking it, but: You and the eminent Briscoe *are* good business partners? That is, you are on the best of terms?"

Fury chuckled. "No, we aren't on the best of terms, but we function together. We disagree on many things, but nothing so serious as to warrant the other's death."

Hung dismissed the subject with an embarrassed flick of his wrist. "Of course not," he laughed softly. "It was foolish of me to ask." He glanced at his watch. "Well," he said, tamping his cigarette out and slapping his hands on his knees, "I'm sure you have plans for the evening and I'm certain I have work to do. I will leave now."

They stood up. "Will you need me in the near future?" asked Fury as he escorted the inspector to the door.

Hung shook his head. "We have your statement, which is all we need for the present. The injured youth will not stand trial for months and your presence is not necessary for levying of charges. I regret the damage to your possessions, and I shall permit the hotel to eradicate all evidence of this incident. Please, enjoy your evening, Mr. Fury. I will assign a plain-clothes guard to this floor for our mutual peace of mind."

Dear Inspector Hung, thought Fury when the door closed behind the policeman, you are a name-dropper. I could have dropped the same names and gotten the same response I'd given you. And everybody was so curious about death, lately.

垂死的星星與赤色巨人

Chapter 8

Conflicting
Purposes

As he buttoned up the formal shirt in front of the bathroom mirror, his mind wandered back over his talk with Hung. On one hand, it was only natural that Hung should show an interest in why he wasn't dead; businessmen *were* usually helpless. But on the other hand, the mention of Bluelist and Briscoe caused a complete reversal in the inspector's attitude; cordial aloofness all the way. Fury was almost disappointed that Hung hadn't continued to hound him for acting so out of character. He couldn't believe that Briscoe's name carried that much weight in Hong Kong, no matter how many times he'd been privy to the Executive Council. In fact, Briscoe's name shouldn't have chased Hung off; if anything, it should have made him more curious.

He supposed Hung would trace the four red dots back to the Gorgon's Head. Then what? See Pok, owner of the restaurant and native son millionaire, just might be questioned about his connection with a secret society supposedly gone commercial instead of criminal. But he could see the investigation going no further than the dark recesses of the Gorgon's Head.

While the hotel's cleaning staff busied themselves restoring the suite, he had tried to run down the mysterious telephone call. No one had called, not Tinto, not Amber, nor even Briscoe. No one he knew had called during the attack. More intriguing was the fact that no one in Colonial Administration had ever heard of Amber Lee. He looked for her number in the Hong Kong telephone directory: no listing there, either.

Fury reached for the band of black, snaked it under his collar, and whipped it into a perfect bow in fifteen seconds. He regarded the total result he saw in the mirror. *That's what stands between Briscoe and Company—a frightening, awesome company—and what?* It was clear now that they wanted him out of the way, at any price, to have access, free and clear, to what was left of his kind of world. *I'm equal to the whole fantastic scheme,* he thought. *It stops here, it stops with me. It always has, hasn't it?* He remembered shocking a priest once in a home for wayward boys when he told him that he didn't care whether a God existed or not, just let Him try and start something. . . .

He wasn't expecting Amber until seven, and no one else at all this evening, so when there was a knock on his door at a quarter to six, his fingers froze on the tie as he was giving it one last pull. Everyone rang up from the desk downstairs first; hotel policy, no exceptions. He went to the bedroom and glanced around for something to take with him to the door. Nothing.

The knock came again. He stepped into the drawing room and settled for the floor lamp that stood next to the red chaise lounge in the corner. He slid off the shade, unplugged the cord and wrapped it around the base, then strode to the door. "Yes, who is it?"

No answer, except a louder, harsher series of raps.

It might be the policeman Hung said he'd station on this floor, and it might not be. To hell with games, Fury decided, easing out the button in the knob to unlock the door and bringing the metal rod of the lamp pole close to the bulb, so that if it was trouble, an upward thrust of his arm would give it a full face of glass.

Just then he felt the knob strain lightly under his hand, the faint vibration of it being tried from the outside. Drawing back the lamp pole, he yanked the door open, and met the wide, startled eyes of Amber staring back at him—and a tiny automatic pointed directly at his stomach.

They both frowned and exclaimed together, "Why didn't you answer?"

And they both stood dumbfounded for a moment, then burst out laughing. Less synchronized, they answered together, "I did! Didn't you hear me?"

When they finished laughing, Fury's features sobered, and he nodded to the gun in her hand. "It doesn't shoot penny candy, I'm sure. What are you doing with it?"

Her finger moved to flick on the safety latch of the gun. "May I come in?" she asked.

He stood aside, then stepped into the corridor and looked up and down. No policeman.

"I told him to take a break," said Amber. "He'll return when he sees us in the lobby."

Fury stepped back inside, rapping the door with his knuckles twice: thick as a brick wall. He closed it, then crossed the room to replace the lamp. "So you *are* with the police," he remarked.

"No," smiled Amber, deftly looping a short black cape from her shoulders and dropping it in one of the chairs. "Do you always greet your guests at the end of an eight foot pole?"

"I was expecting an encore of this afternoon's funny business," he said, slipping the shade back on. "And you're early. Do you always come calling with a gun?"

"No . . . When I didn't hear your answer, I thought the worst."

He turned to face her. "You *are* aware of what happened here?"

"Yes. You don't mind, do you?" She leaned to one side, her hands poised gracefully on one hip in a perfect model's pose. She'd rearranged her hair, bringing it up into a haughty Gibson bouffant. She wore black high heels, black sleeve gloves, and a black, sleeveless, silk Chinese gown, sleek and shimmering, that was slit at one leg midway up her outer thigh. The next thing he noticed was her neck—thin, slender and unadorned, set in a kind of Delhi half-collar that diminished to a point between her breasts. There, suspended from an incredibly fine, almost invisible gold chain from around her neck, was a wafer-thin jade disk of soft, lustrous amber.

Suddenly he was there with her, kissing her gently on the lips and brushing his cheek lightly against her scented hair. He felt her encircle him with her arms in a tightness that meant more than affection, and lay her head on his shoulder and sigh heavily. He held her away from him a little, so that she would have to face him. "How could you know what happened, Amber? I can't imagine there's a police wire in your economics section."

She disengaged herself from him, then sat down on one of the chairs and took a cigarette from her little pearl gray, oblong purse, fitted it into a holder of similar color, and lit it with a tiny gold lighter. She leaned back and crossed her legs, daringly exposing the one with the slit. A pleased smile grew on her mouth as she watched Fury's face harden. "I was so informed," she said.

"By Inspector Hung?"

"Perhaps."

"How do you rank in the scheme of things that you can tell an officer of the law to take a break?"

"You're in a questionable mood tonight," she said teasingly.

"Perhaps I ought to go home."

"You have no such intention," said Fury, reaching for the gun, which she'd laid on the coffee table next to her purse. "You still haven't explained what you're doing with this." Fury weighed the thing in the palm of his hand; it couldn't have been more than a pound, he estimated. And he couldn't see it being accurate over fifty feet; he doubted if it could stop a mouse at ten. There were no markings or numbers on it anywhere. It was of a design and make he'd never seen before.

She watched him examine the gun, then answered, "I brought it because I thought it wiser to have some protection than none. Because . . . of what happened here today."

"Nothing happened to *me*, Amber," he said. "You should have been so informed." He inserted his trigger finger through the guard; it was as tight as a ring. He shook his head dubiously, then laid the gun back on the table and sat next to her. "You still haven't answered my question."

"But I have. You're in danger. You need a bodyguard. Isn't that plausible enough?"

"It would be if I knew why *you're* so certain I need one."

She turned and faced him. "Merritt, please don't be angry with me. There are many things I can't tell you, now or ever. I know how you feel. And I want to tell you. But for both our goods it's better that I don't. You can ask as much as you like; I can't promise you the truth."

Fury studied her for a moment, then said, "Of this I'm sure: You're not just a lady who collects economic statistics for a government bureau."

"No. I'm a lady who makes sense of them."

"I'm not a statistic likely to come by your desk."

She put her cigarette down and settled closer to him. "No," she said, running her fingers through the hair on the back of his head, "you're not a statistic. And you're not a consumer, or a person, or a 'people,' or any of those things. You're a man. And you *did* come by my desk . . . and I've loved you ever since."

He ran the back of his hand up the side of her face. "And you engineered the dinner last night, too."

"No. That was pure good fortune. But you were right; we *would* have met sooner or later. I'd have made sure of it." She leaned closer and tickled his ear with her tongue.

He sighed, pushed her gently away, and stood up. Noticing the gun on the table again, he picked it up, looked at her purse, and then at her. It certainly wouldn't fit in her purse, and her gown didn't lend itself to concealment. "If you're my body-guard," he chuckled, "then where do you pack this?"

She stood up and took the gun from him, then planted her un-slitted leg on the coffee table and swept away the gown. There, serving in place of a garter for her nylons, was a wide band of elastic supporting a little holster on her inside thigh. She slipped the automatic in and snapped the guard strap over it.

He didn't need to reach far. Fury held her close, almost crushing her, not letting her alter that pose, and kissed her long and hard and deep. Her mouth answered in kind, as did her hips, pressing against him in sustained, provocative yearning. He tore his mouth from hers and studied her face. He smiled at the closed eyes. "You planned that, too."

She shook her head slowly, and said, "You're a dream to predict. Open as a book." Then she brought around one hand and traced a gloved finger over the pulsating vein on his fore-head. "Didn't you hear me the first time, Merritt?" she whispered. "I love you." She saw in his strained but unyielding stare the answer that he had heard, and she saw a desire to answer in kind.

Fury flexed his hands on her shoulder blades. *"I* can't say that yet, Amber."

"I know," she sighed, resting her head on his shoulder. "And I know you. It isn't plausible that anyone could love you as is, is it?" She lifted her head and studied his attentive face. "*As is,* isn't it, love? No watered-stock for you, isn't that right? You care too much for what you can feel, and I understand that. It doesn't matter that you can't say that to me now, love. I've waited this long, too. I know why you can't say it. . . ."

"I can say this, Amber: You don't conflict with my purposes."

She took her leg from the table and smoothed down her gown. "Finish dressing," she smiled, reaching for her purse and taking out some lipstick.

Fury watched her snap open a compact mirror and run a lipstick over her lips. "I'm also sure," he added, "that if the need arises, you'll draw attention quicker than you will that gun."

✻   ✻   ✻   ✻   ✻

After dinner at *La Lumière à la Fin du Monde,* as they idled over drinks at their little corner table, Amber abruptly broke their conversation on the economics of Hong Kong with the question, "Have you ever wondered what people mean when they ask you to 'reach out'? It isn't a phrase repeated often here. But I notice it a lot in American advertising copy. It's suspicious."

Fury, though taken aback, was amused. "No, not for a long time. I've discovered that people who ask that of one usually learn that there's nothing in themselves for one to reach for. Then they become very violent." He paused. "How can that have anything to do with the issue of Hong Kong versus the G.A.T.T.?"

"Because the onus of initiation—of 'reaching out'—always seems to fall on those who have something. It's never the other way around."

Fury shrugged. "It usually is with a swindle, or a con-job. And while one is reaching out, someone is reaching in—either for your wallet, or your soul."

"It smacks of slumming," said Amber. "I never thought highly of slummers or of people who like being slummed on."

Fury laughed. "I stand corrected. There *is* a connection between that and Hong Kong versus the G.A.T.T."

Amber said, "I was curious to see how long it would take you to realize that. Merritt, love, there's nothing unfinished in you."

"May I return the compliment?" Fury paused. "You have another admirer, you know."

"One is enough, thank you."

"There's a man over there in the corner, beneath the bust of Raffles, and he's paying us far more attention than he is his dinner."

Amber turned discreetly, then faced Fury again, a small but firm frown on her mouth. She reached for her cigarettes and took one out of the pack. Fury lit it. "Merritt," she said, "you must move out of that hotel."

"I don't think Briscoe will try anything else there again."

"You can move in with me for the duration of your stay."

"Thank you, I will." Fury glanced at the man in the far corner again, then said, "He shares many of my features. Could very well be my older brother, if I had one. He's even wearing the same cut of tux . . . smokes Rothmans . . . uses a gold Dunhill lighter . . . Or is it a DuPont, can't tell from here. . . . Anyway, he looks more monied than either of us . . . Wonder what his business is?"

And later, as they danced in the ballroom of an exclusive hotel overlooking Repulse Bay, Fury said softly in Amber's ear, "Do you think it's coincidence or destiny that two people like us—with so much in common—should ever meet?"

Amber lifted her head and frowned incredulously. "What

an unnecessary question!" she admonished. "That sounded like a question sent to Miss Shu's Wailing World Love Column and Homemaker's Guide."

"Three, then?" chuckled Fury.

"Merritt, you are making little sense."

Fury guided her back across the floor to their table. "Our admirer is sitting just three tables from us, Amber, and he's wearing a gun, which I noticed when he raised his left arm to signal a waiter. It's either that or he has an usually developed left triceps and a special tailor."

A shadow of a frown tightened Amber's forehead. "I know," she answered in a moment.

Fury held her eyes. "Is he one of yours?"

"He's . . . from the Foreign Office," she answered tentatively. "A protocol officer. He's here to see that things are done right with Lon Ping."

After another moment, Fury asked, "Did he arrange Ping's trip to Bluelist today?"

Amber's hand clutched hard at his on the table, and her eyes flared. *"Why didn't you tell me earlier??"*

"I thought you knew why the Dying Stars paid me a visit today," said Fury.

"No," she said, shaking her head. "He doesn't arrange *those* things. He . . . he does his own. . . ." Her words trailed off. "I . . . I thought it was Briscoe, too. . . ."

"Briscoe came out with Pok and Lon Ping, who was apparently introduced to Ushio and a British construction engineer by the name of Rutledge, as Pan Chao, of Felicity Bank. Then I entered the lie. Ping hasn't wasted any time seeing to his realm, has he?"

"No," said Amber. "But he won't waste any more time on Bluelist. He has a dozen things to keep him busy, besides diplomacy."

"Closer and closer to the truth come I," said Fury. He lit a cigarette. "What did Briscoe do in the war, Amber? I bought a little book yesterday that mentions names and dates but nothing specific."

Amber looked away from him.

"Amber," said Fury, "I know you're in this up to your neck. *I'm* in it up to my neck. But it's *my* neck that's on the block, apparently. You owe me some of the truth."

Amber said, after a moment, "Briscoe helped return Cossack army units to the Soviets after Germany fell. Then he traced German scientists in hiding and gave them to the Soviets, too. Some of the people he tracked down were not scientists, but just refugees or dissidents. They were simply killed."

"I see," said Fury.

"Merritt," said Amber, getting up, "I must meet that man in the corner, and then make a phone call. Pay the check and meet me outside in five minutes."

Before Fury could reply, she was gone.

Outside, they waited while the doorman called for his MGB. As he tipped the doorman and the parking attendant, Fury glanced over and noticed Amber fingering the disk that hung from her neck—and the handsome stranger standing near her, but watching him, instead.

"Not so fast," said Amber when they were in the MGB. "I don't want to lose him. And, Merritt—don't interfere."

Fury eased his foot off the accelerator and asked, "Where are we going?"

"Not far from here. A park. Just stay on this road. I'll tell you when to stop."

He saw the lights of a car following them not far behind in the rear-view mirror. Amber's sight was fixed rigidly on the winding road ahead. Fury asked, "Don't interfere in what, Amber? What is going to transpire between you two?"

She turned her head slowly to him. A car passed them going in the other direction, and her eyes flashed once. "Your future," she said.

They stopped near a dark stand of pines nearly two miles from the hotel. A green Porsche pulled up and stopped ten feet behind them. Fury judged that they were in the center of the island. A Toyota whizzed by in the direction of Repulse Bay.

"Don't get out," said Amber, a sharp edge in her words. "Just do as I say." She lifted one of her legs, reached under the gown, and took out the gun. Then she was out of the car and striding back to the Porsche.

Fury turned in his seat in time to see the stranger climb out to meet her. They both stood and stared back at him. Fury heard her say distinctly in the still night air, "There he is. Don't make a mess of it. I'll get rid of the car myself."

The man glanced at her once, then reached inside his jacket and produced an automatic. He moved closer to Fury casually, almost indifferently. Fury watched with fascination as the man stopped near the trunk and raised his gun.

But the stony confidence in the man's face flew apart in surprise and pain as two quick shots snapped from behind him. He sunk to his knees, then pivoted feebly with one leg half raised to face Amber with his gun. Not moving, she fired once more, almost point-blank into his face. The man jerked, then slumped forward.

Amber swept her gown aside, strapped in her gun, then rushed back to the MGB. Before Fury could open his door she was back in beside him. Headlights suddenly swung around a bend in the direction of Repulse Bay and bore down on them. It was the Toyota. It pulled up behind the Porsche and honked twice. "Go!" said Amber.

Fury shifted angrily, stepped on the gas, and they went. As the wind streamed by them, he said, "Explanation—and none of this damned secrecy!"

Amber lit them both a cigarette. "He was to have been your executioner," she said quietly.

"I see," replied Fury, taking the cigarette. "He does his own. For the Foreign Office. I didn't know murder was an item of protocol."

"He was in Hong Kong for two weeks and that was his cover. We knew what he was but didn't know why he was here. Not until three days ago, before you and the others arrived. He . . . he thought I was setting you up for him."

"'We'—does that include the Toyota?"

"The clean-up squad. They'll drive Mr. Carlton and the Porsche to a cliff somewhere and run them over it."

"Why didn't he try for me sooner?"

"He did. With the Dying Stars, apparently. He must have been under a lot of pressure to try and do it that way. Probably from Pok. He'd been following you since your meeting yesterday. I didn't know he would want to . . . kill you so soon."

"And what exactly is—or was—his connection with Briscoe?"

Amber did not answer immediately. "You'll find out soon enough on your own, Merritt. I can't tell you any more than that. Just understand that Carlton was here to 'handle' you or Ronquillo or Ushio or Derek had any of you elected not to leave the partnership. And understand that what happened back there was the culmination of a year's work. Bluelist goes back much farther."

"What is it they want to hide, Amber?"

"You must learn that for yourself, Merritt."

"And when I do?"

"Act on what you know."

"That's all?"

Amber swept her head around. He saw an intense, tortured worship in her eyes. She said nothing.

"What is it *you're* hiding, Amber?" he asked.

"Nothing important, love," she whispered, shaking her head. "Nothing important."

Fury pulled over to the side of the road, on the edge of a cliff that overlooked Wanchai, and killed the motor. He leaned over and rested a hand on the nape of her neck. Above them, the searchlights from Victoria Peak, two silent but clashing broadswords of white, careened and cut across the sky. "Should I thank you for saving my life—or for endangering it?" he asked.

"I think I should thank you for having one worth saving."

He studied her face for a moment. "I won't bother you with any more questions—for now." He smiled. "You couldn't conflict with my purposes."

"Don't go back to the hotel. . . . You've been moved from there already. To my place. You can't be traced now."

"I have business to conduct," he said.

"Go about it, then," she answered. "You don't conflict with my purposes, either."

"How many times have you had to use that gun?"

"As many times as has been necessary."

"You don't regret it?"

"No."

Fury reached over with his other hand and picked the amber disk from between her breasts, then bent and pressed his lips to it.

*   *   *   *   *

He marvelled at the efficiency with which he had been moved from the Mandarin. Everything of his was in her apartment and in its logical place. When he asked her how it was possible for a guest to be moved out over the possible objections of hotel management, she smiled and said, "Perhaps it was possible that the hotel had no objections."

He noticed her apartment for the first time. Over a bookcase was a framed color print of the *Blue Monkey* of Thera, a fragment of decorative wall art discovered some years ago by archaeologists on the remains of a Greek island that had blown up over two thousand years ago. Blue on blue; it was the most relaxing mix of shades he'd ever seen. On another shelf was a porcelain vase, over two feet high, of different shades of bright blue and white and copper-red, depicting two Oriental dragons chasing some round flaming objects in the sky and through swirling blue water. The meaning of it was lost on him, but Oriental colors rarely failed to attract and soothe his eye.

"It's from the Ch'ien Lung period," Amber said, coming up from behind him. "It's almost two hundred years old. Ch'ien Lung—he was the last real Emperor of China, and old when your ancestors were putting holes in the British ranks on Bunker Hill."

"Breed's Hill," corrected Fury with a smile.

"He refused to establish formal relations with Britain because its envoy refused to *kowtow* to him."

"Admirable enemies all around, back then," remarked Fury, reaching up and stroking a side of the vase.

"You shouldn't touch it," said Amber, laying a hand on his arm. "It's very valuable and handling it won't tell you anything about it that you don't already know—that it's beautiful and unique and serene."

Fury turned to her and held her shoulders instead. "Some beautiful and unique things can't be fully appreciated unless they're handled."

Much later, Fury gently locked an arm around her neck on the pillow and kissed her ear. "There's something funny happening in your Secret Service, isn't there?"

He felt her stiffen, then chuckle lazily.

"Tell me about Briscoe, then," he continued, winding a length of her hair around his finger.

Amber sighed, then relaxed. "He learned his Chinese—both Mandarin and Cantonese—at Cambridge, Peking and Canton.

When this mission finally came up—that of establishing amicable ties with Peking—he was to become a millionaire and a
success story and to develop the strongest commercial ties possible. He almost failed. A half dozen of his business schemes
failed miserably, but he had a portion of the Secret Service
budget backing him up, plus the generous terms of a small
commercial bank in London that is really a government operation."

"Regency Road?" suggested Fury.

"Yes. How did you know?"

"A directory of local hongs I found in an old book shop."

"He finally did it in bamboo and lumber. He sells to Hong
Kong, Japan, Taiwan, and Australia. But he's also Peking's
petty cash bursar—in gold. He isn't involved in the big buying
and selling on the open market, he merely helps finance sub-
versive activities in this area and acts as an economic consultant
for Peking when it wants to place a large amount of money.
He's helped them take over or buy control of many banks,
businesses, and even what unions there are here."

"Did Kwong Lai object?"

"No," said Amber, nestling her head more comfortably in
the angle of his bent arm, "he was too enthusiastic and brought
them attention they didn't want. He was gotten rid of."

"And Chan Ha Tze?"

"He *did* object. He was a refugee from across the border
who appreciated the difference in lives he led here and in
China. He was the only member of his family to escape alive.
And he was no fool. When he was hired as an officer of Felicity he soon grasped what was being done. He contacted us, and
became one of our most important sources of information."

"Until it was learned that he had a friend at Colonial Administration, and Felicity decided to float a loan for the fish."
Fury paused. "You didn't offer him any protection?"

"We didn't know he was under suspicion. When the police

inquired, we learned that they had rigged an embezzlement scandal to explain his death."

Fury sighed. "Amber, of what use is intelligence—your kind of information, I mean—if you don't use it?"

She answered a long moment later, turning in his embrace to face him. "We kill only when there has been a killing, or when we know there will be one. We had no incontestable proof of Briscoe or Pok having ordered those men's deaths." She paused. "We have had study projects on men like Briscoe and Pok, and Pelosi. When we have sound evidence that they have resorted to killing to establish their power, we dissolve their power. Their killing justifies their own deaths. If there has been no killing, we cannot act. It means that men don't mind becoming slaves, or peons, or coolies, or 'persons.' . . ."

"Then what are you waiting for?"

Amber smiled. "Someone like you. Someone who welcomes the chance to defy the world. Someone who knows there is no difference between living his life gloriously and dying gloriously for the right to live that life untouched." Amber brought his head down and kissed him longingly.

Fury broke her hold and looked at her shrewdly. "*Do* you have a job at Government House?"

Amber laughed. "You promised—no more questions!"

Fury grunted, and drew her closer to him. "Palm reader, bodyguard, seductress, economist, spy, hit man, and piecemeal dispenser of truth. I fall in love with the strangest women."

Amber moaned, and, pressing her face closer, bit into the side of his neck.

目的衝突

Chapter 9

Think
Chocolates

When he woke, Amber was gone. He found a note in her kitchen: "Be cautious. Briscoe and Pok have flown to Singapore for the day. You may visit Bluelist without worry, but be *cautious!* Avoid crowds. I must go to work. I kissed you goodbye, but you never noticed. Love, Amber."

Fury chuckled to himself. Well, he was going to Bluelist's offices this morning anyway. Briscoe or no Briscoe. They'd hardly try a broad daylight ploy in so public a place.

He called Tinto first, gave him his new number, and agreed to two appointments in the afternoon. One was with Paul Chan, of whom the Japanese sung praises. Then he called Bluelist and asked to speak to Harry Briscoe. No, sir, Mr. Briscoe will be unavailable for appointments until tomorrow. Do you know where I can reach him? It's quite urgent. No, sir, he is in Singapore, but I do not know his number. Thank you, I'll call tomorrow.

He climbed into the MGB at nine-thirty, wondering how he was going to follow Amber's advice and avoid crowds in Hong Kong. Ten minutes later he parked it in a garage a block away and walked to Bluelist's offices. It was one of those bright, sunny, infectious mornings and he was whistling as he stepped out of the elevator and into the lobby. He stopped when he noticed that Bluelist's name had been removed from beneath that of the Shota Trading Company's on the glass door.

Ushio's secretary said Jumpei wasn't in. "He called this morning and said he was not feeling well and was only going to Granite Island," she told Fury. "He said to route any important calls to him there."

Fury grunted in surprise. Granite Island was one of a cluster of small uninhabited islands called the Ninepin Group, several miles southeast of Hong Kong. Shota Trading had a granite quarry there and ferried out crews three or four times a week. It was not a trip one made if one weren't feeling well. He asked, "You're sure it was Mr. Ushio?"

The woman giggled. "Yes, of course. It was on the recorder this morning." She giggled again. "He *sounded* sick," she said. *"Saki* sick."

Fury grinned at her mischief and gossip-filled eyes. *"Is* there a shift today on Granite?" he asked.

"No," said the secretary. She leaned forward and spoke in confidence. "I do not really think he went there today," she whispered. "He does not want to be disturbed. Saki headaches are the worst ones if one is not a regular saki drinker. This has happened before."

"Oh? When?"

"When he was promoted from manager to partner."

"Well," sighed Fury, "if he happens to call, tell him I'm here and would like to speak with him. It's urgent. I'll be in the library."

"Yes, Mr. Fury."

Well, he'd do it himself. In the library was a special cabinet for geological maps. Fury set his briefcase down, went to it, ran his finger down the Japanese-English labels, then rolled out a drawer and pulled out a bound volume of twenty maps labeled,

"Tungsten and Cassiterite Deposits: South China & Australasia Regions."

At a table, he opened it, flipped through a few of the massive pages, and found what he was looking for. He'd done this same thing before a year ago, but for a completely different reason.

Bluelist Number Four was one dot at the southernmost portion of an enormous cluster of dots that formed a kind of ellipse, the bulk of which lay inside Red China in Kwangtung and Kiangsi provinces, just north of the New Territories. There were about fifty dots, perhaps sixty percent of them yellow, which the legend at the bottom of the page indicated were rich deposits. Blues were marginal, and browns sub-marginal. Bluelist, of course, was a blue dot, clearly circled in red pencil.

It needed only one glance to understand why tungsten prices had gone haywire. The *Commodities Quotation* reported Asian tungsten up twenty-five points above the pre-Senate study announcement level. Stateside stocks had gone through the floor and the new Commodities Exchange Commission had ordered a price ceiling on all tungsten trading. Ushio said that Red China produced the most and best high-grade tungsten, and what little it was able to produce went mostly to Europe. But given the chance—given the means—given a little help from its friends, it could swamp the market and name its own terms, which, coming from Peking via Briscoe and Bluelist, wouldn't be cheap.

Distractedly, Fury glanced at his watch; he had about two hours before his appointment with Chan in Kowloon. He opened his briefcase and took out a notebook. He guessed he could write a thorough sketch of the prospect of a Peking corner of tungsten in an hour or so. Five minutes later he was engrossed in his task.

"Curiosity killed the cat."

Fury looked up. Harry Briscoe stood in the doorway.

Briscoe smiled apologetically. "Excuse the mundane expression, but I couldn't think of another so aptly suited to this occasion."

Fury grimaced. "You're supposed to be in Singapore."

"Delayed flight," said Briscoe lightly. "Which was quite fortunate. Forgot some paperwork of mine."

"You'd better see to it then, Harry," said Fury. "I have work to do."

"Of course. Won't be a minute," said Briscoe, turning.

"Take your time."

Briscoe laughed amiably. "*My* time, old friend? Why, not at all!"

Fury lit a cigarette and pondered Briscoe's presence, then shrugged. If he tried any nonsense here, he'd be out of his mind. Too many of Ushio's people were around. Fury devoted one last draught of his cigarette to the subject, then concentrated on the map. He soon lost track of time, his own and anybody else's.

Forty-five minutes later he pocketed his pen and glanced once again at his notes. All he had to do was show it to Amber. Then she'd have as good a picture of the situation as he did.

Briscoe chose to walk back in then. He closed the library door and leaned back on it. "You have a lot of gall, Fury," he smiled. "But what I really think is that your intimacy with the mentally deranged is not limited to mere observation." His glance danced briefly on the maps. "It won't do you a bit of good, you know. I told you not to bother yourself."

Fury merely sat with his arms folded, staring at Briscoe thoughtfully.

Briscoe came closer and sat on the edge of the table. He said, with a sad note in his voice, "It's beyond your scope of action, your capacity to stop."

"Don't count on it," answered Fury, shaking his head. "It probably means I'll have to deal with you as I've dealt with your proxies."

Briscoe nodded. "And very ably dealt with, too. But don't blame me for the Dying Stars, Merritt. That was Pok's idea. He always had a sense of the melodramatic. Carlton was more my style. You remember him? I don't imagine you were introduced, though. It's too bad he had to be sacrificed."

"You haven't seen Jumpei since we parted yesterday, have you, Harry?"

Briscoe smiled wanly and replied casually, "I met with him for drinks last night. Why do you ask?"

"He didn't know that was really Lon Ping yesterday."

Briscoe chuckled. "So we learned. But he would have in due time, through you or someone else. I don't think he'll be in today. Stomach cramps, splitting headache. He complained of them so volubly he depressed us." Briscoe's smile widened, elevating his moustache a full inch. "Comes from looking at a Gorgon's Head, you know. What was its name? Medusa, wasn't it?"

Fury said, "Isn't your analogy wrong, Harry? Medusa turned men into stone. One would have stomach cramps from trying to ingest certain ceremonial knives."

"No," chuckled Briscoe. "I understand Jumpei paid a visit to his granite quarry. Had an accident with the crusher, I believe. Inhaled too much granite dust. Some men can't be trusted to turn to stone when they see things they shouldn't."

"How are you going to explain *his* murder?"

Briscoe's face wrinkled in incredulity, and he shrugged. "Me? It has nothing to do with me, my friend. I expect the quarry supervisor will have a bloody mess to report when he and his crew go out tomorrow morning. All I can do is send condolences to his home office. I'd ask you to help me pick out the appropriate card, but I fear you won't be in the mood. And I don't think I'll be meeting Jumpei's replacement, either. Bluelist will have moved out of here by the end of the week."

"Bluelist is a front," stated Fury.

"Bluelist and everything that will follow it are things I planned and plotted for much too hard and for too long to allow some wet-behind-the-ears boy scout walk in and arrest it all with his bloody scruples."

"Planning and plotting since Regency Road Bank?"

Briscoe looked at Fury with amazement. He slid off the table and sat down opposite. "Curious remark number two," he said, his eyes scintillating with the humor of somebody paid a surprise compliment. "There was the one yesterday to Pok about the Houghton-Devane Group. Now this one. Things that are not general knowledge."

"Regency Road Bank is a member of the Houghton-Devane Group, isn't it?"

"Correct."

Fury risked a conjecture. "Regency Road is a government bank, fronting as a private bank. It was founded with government money, perhaps in the 'Fifties, and you were one of its first officers. It's a covert instrument of foreign policy. It initiates and finances investment schemes no private bank in its right mind would touch. All of its foreign policy-motivated deals are underwritten by either the Treasury or the Exchequer. Possibly by both. But it *has* fallen into bad times."

Briscoe reached out and helped himself to one of Fury's Rothmans. He laughed, then shook his head. "This *is* curious. Who are you, Merritt—*really?* Here I sit, having a cordial chat with an otherwise admirable and likeable young man, when off rolls his tongue one of the most eyes-only operations in recent history." He paused and leaned forward. "So secret and so smoothly run to date that we doubted American knowledge of it. Not even our Commonwealth cousins are privy to it. Don't tell me the Yanks are working at cross purposes, too?"

"Some are, Harry," smiled Fury, lighting another Rothman. "Tell me if I'm wrong," he said. "Skipping over how long it took you to do it and how, you and See Pok and perhaps Walter Pelosi are about to corner the world market in tungsten." He reached out and drew the maps over. Using his pen as a pointer, he continued. "You'll take all you can handle from Kiangsi, Hunan and Kwangtung provinces in Red—" he paused to grin emphatically at Briscoe here—"*Red* China, funnel it out through the new Bluelist port facility on Tolo Channel, and ship it anywhere you please. No one will be the wiser. You can claim the tungsten came from anywhere in the Far East. Or perhaps you won't need to cover anything up, neither your role nor the source of the ore." He paused. "People don't blush as much as they used to in the company of killers."

Briscoe shook his head in mock disgust. "Fickle people."

Fury went on. "Of course, your biggest market will be the States. And in Europe there are plenty of potential customers who'll do anything to keep their steel industries going. Look at what they did to Japan—practically shut it out of the market because its steel was too good and too cheap. But—I don't think you'd have gambled the amount of time and money you and your backers must have put into this scheme, if you weren't assured a captive market, one made captive by Walter Pelosi and friends."

Briscoe studied Fury for a moment. "I'll say it again, my friend: You have a disproportionate share of gall." He winked. "And of intelligence, too. I'm sure I'm glad it can't be rationed among the general public. I've woolled the eyes of some of the best Far East traders alive. What put you on to me?"

Fury grinned. "You, Harry. You and the fact that one of the best Far East traders alive expressed an inordinate interest in as worthless a property as Bluelist." He waved his pen and tapped the map with it. "You could market North Korean tungsten, too, I notice. Let's see. Rail lines are sparse throughout Kwangtung and Kiangsi, so the ore taken out of those provinces would have to be trucked to Ch'ang Sha, or Leiyang,

or Chu-t'ing, points on the Canton-Kowloon rail line. Would-
n't be too big a project building a spur from there to Bluelist
and Tolo. No problem at all for a firm like Matheson and
Tuttle, heady from a building binge in the Middle East. As for
the North Korean ore—well, that would have to be freighted
from their port of Chongjul on the Yellow Sea . . . here . . .
straight to Shanghai . . . here . . . then by rail through China to
Canton . . . then on down to Kowloon." Fury paused. "That's
if you wanted to disguise its source. If not, North Korean
freighters—probably built by and leased from Pok—could call
in plain sight on Hong Kong and your busy little multi-million
dollar refining complex." Fury, satisfied, dropped the pen on a
conclusive note.

Briscoe nodded his head in appreciation.

Fury continued. "What do the North Koreans produce?
About eight percent of the world production? Red China? At
present, about sixteen percent. The States? About fifteen percent. But that won't be the case if the Bookin-Denning bill
passes. Will it, Harry?"

Briscoe shook his head in agreement.

Fury closed the volume sharply and shoved it away. "Of
course, we mustn't forget the Soviet Union: over twenty-two
percent. The rest can't count; they're mostly state-run mines
too with no rhyme or reason to their operations. They'll either
close down altogether or make a market-slice deal with the major. What will the Soviets do? They have Eastern Europe sewn
up and even have an established position in Western Europe.
Then who *will* be the major?" Fury paused. "That all depends
on who has a corner on the States. I can't at this moment predict the outcome of that bidding session, but I can guarantee
that everybody's shill will be running around, handing out fa-
vors and making deals and spending tons of money in and
around the Potomac."

Briscoe raised his brow. "I believe I have read somewhere

that influence-peddling is fast becoming an important American service industry," he remarked with affected indolence.

"That's about it, Harry. That's how the Arabs and all the other newly-hatched have done it. Well, actually, they didn't *do* anything. Oil and copper and uranium were handed to them in much the same fashion as tungsten can be handed to the Soviets and Peking."

After a moment, Briscoe shook his head. "Why *did* you bother, Merritt?" he asked with genuine, concerned interest. "What could be your antipathy for it?"

"Write it off to inveterate contrariness," smiled Fury.

"Out to save the world?"

"Hardly. I rarely concern myself with suicides—except when they want to take me with them. In this case that only happens to include the world; I can't do anything about that."

"You really know how not to flatter a person."

"Flattery can be a form of inflation, and equally unjust."

Briscoe looked solemn. "There's nothing you can do to stop it, you know. It's going to happen sooner or later. It's in the cards, as you Americans would put it. Look at your own country. It's already half-way down the yellow brick road to state economic management and guaranteed incomes and all the other frauds one can expect in such situations." He shook his head. "Don't you see? Most people today have stopped concerning themselves with freedom and justice and all the other hallucinations and begun worrying about the power they think they should have to protect themselves from the ones who already have it. It's a macabre circus, isn't it? It's also a demonstrable fact of history. Give an inch and someone's bound to take over—sooner or later. The power is either there for the taking or it isn't. If frightened little milquetoasts like our mutual partner Walter Pelosi can have access to mean little fools like Senators Bookin and Denning, who happen to have the power and the glory, then it *must* happen. If it weren't for the power, all the milquetoasts and fools would have nothing better to do than pump petrol at filling stations or run second-rate haberdasheries."

"Does our toy dealer know that you're a British agent really working for Peking?"

"Hasn't the foggiest," chuckled Briscoe. "He suspects something, but he'd really rather not know. He's so unlike you, Merritt. In fact, before we convened the last meeting of Bluelist, I asked him to stay at my house on Repulse Bay instead of a hotel. I didn't want to risk any of the ex-partners calling on him and asking him a lot of unsettling questions. Derek can be abusive and Bernardo absolutely frightening. You? I think you'd fairly wring his neck."

"No. Just break it."

"You *do* want to stop me, don't you? Why? What would it get you? That is, to put it in a more grammatically correct form, what tangible benefit could you possibly incur by trying to stop something that *must* happen, whether through me or anybody else?" Briscoe paused. "Are you perhaps jealous that there isn't any room for you in my future?"

"Jealous, Harry?" chuckled Fury. "No. We'd bang heads in the best of worlds."

Briscoe laughed. "I must agree with you there, Merritt. Then why?"

"My reasons wouldn't interest you, Harry. They have to do with flags and ideas and whatever else you'd call an hallucination." Fury paused. "What's in it for *you?*"

Briscoe watched as Fury rose and put his things back inside the briefcase. "Oh," he shrugged tentatively, "another decoration, I suppose. A baronetcy, with an estate to match. That, and a few tax exemptions of my choice. All on the sly, though. The Opposition back home wouldn't take kindly to it. They raised the devil when I got my K.C.M.G. Well, what the hell? They can't say much about it now without breaking Official

Secrets and causing more of a row than they'd be able to handle."

Fury snapped the briefcase shut. "A row about all the Cossacks and Germans you handed over to the Soviets?"

Briscoe's brow knotted. "There you go again. Well, after all, there weren't enough Russian goon squads to go around, you know. Poppa Joe asked his Allies for a favor. I was part of that favor. Least we could do." Briscoe snorted. "I've always suspected the reasons behind my ribbons. I expect they were a bribe not to talk. Well, *I* won't. It's not *my* reputation."

Fury stared at Briscoe for a moment, then swung his briefcase from the table to his side. "If they'd give it to a group of shaggy dog songsters, they'd give it to anybody." He smiled at Briscoe's suddenly flushed face, and added, "Gratitude comes so cheaply these days."

Briscoe stood up. "Don't go sanctimonious on me, my young friend. You Yanks had a hand in the great round-up, too."

"Not this Yank, Harry." Fury glanced at his watch. "You'll excuse me now, but I have several appointments this afternoon."

Briscoe regarded Fury as he walked to the door. "I could have been a great fan of yours, Merritt," he said. "I'm sorry we must part this way."

Fury smiled. "You can have my autograph later, Harry. Good day."

✼   ✼   ✼   ✼   ✼

When the elevator doors opened on the ground floor, Fury half expected to be cornered and kidnapped by some of Briscoe's less fond acquaintances. But there was no one waiting for him in the alcove, which led to the corridor that ran straight through the building to connect Jaffe and Lockhart. Nobody except a woman in a cream-colored pantsuit and wide-brimmed hat, watching people rush by.

Fury stepped out of the elevator alcove and rounded the corner, then stopped when he spotted two tough, muscular-looking Chinese lounging on the polish of a gray Rolls parked on Lockhart right at the end of the corridor. The Rolls was Briscoe's, and he recognized one of the men as Briscoe's chauffeur. He turned and walked the other way, towards Jaffe.

He hadn't gone ten steps when two men rounded the corner ahead. One of them had a ten-year-old boy by the neck and was pushing him ahead roughly. There were tears in the boy's eyes; the grip on him must have been terrific. They stopped a few yards away from him and glanced beyond Fury's shoulder. He turned and saw Briscoe by the elevator.

"Accompany my friends, Merritt," he said, "or both you and the boy die instantly. The boy first, with a broken neck. Then you, a bullet in your gut."

Fury said, "I know you mean it, Harry. You've had so much experience." Before he could get Briscoe's reaction, he turned and headed for the gray Rolls. The two men lounging on it came to life, one running around to get into the back seat on the street side, and the other rushing to have the door open for him. When Fury was inside, the second Chinese sat beside him, rocking the vehicle as he fell into the seat.

In front, the driver's door opened and the man who had been holding the boy slipped behind the wheel. Fury saw the boy running hard back down the corridor, screaming his lungs out.

On his left was the chauffeur, sitting placidly, the two biggest, thickest hands Fury had ever seen, planted on his knees. Both men wore dark, somber suits reminiscent of funeral parlors, and had blank obedient faces that smiled much and said nothing.

The passenger door in front opened, then another, more

elderly, more intelligent-looking Chinese bounced in, followed by a beaming Harry Briscoe, who pushed the glass partition open and exclaimed, "What an operation! We'd make a great team, Merritt! Thanks ever so much for walking right into it."

The Rolls surged forward. Briscoe slung an arm over the back of the seat comfortably. He smiled again at Fury, then glanced at his companions and gave a sharp order in Chinese.

The one on Fury's left gently removed the cigarette from Fury's fingers and snuffed it out carefully in the tray on the door, then laid his massive paws on Fury's wrists and yanked them up. The one on his right did the search, patting here and there with deft, gentler hands. In less than half a minute he reached into Fury's coat and lifted out the little automatic Amber had given him, leaving the wallet behind.

Briscoe took the gun and nodded to the other to release Fury's hands. "This is what you did Carlton in with, eh?" He shook his head. "Really, Merritt, don't you know these are against the *law?*" He turned to the elderly Chinese in the middle and gave him the gun. "You'll tell us how you bested Carlton, Merritt. But not now. I'll listen to the tape." He said nothing more as the Rolls dove into the Cross Harbour Tunnel.

The roaring tunnel caused an enforced silence that was habitual, not necessary; the acoustical engineering of the Rolls could bar most outside sounds and inside muffle the movement of a watch. But the abrupt quiet allowed Fury to breathe an inward sigh of relief and time to think. The two gentlemen sitting on either side of him each weighed at least three times more than either of the bellhops, and were more likely to be members of an international wrestling society than of some criminal Boy Scout troop. He glanced at the faces of his companions; both were staring straight ahead at the traffic over the Rolls' hood, and made no effort to look back at him.

Harry Briscoe and the bright sunlight at the end of the

tunnel broke Fury's train of thought. "You have no cause for humor," he said. "Or have you concocted a daring escape?"

Fury tempered his smile. "Memory Lane," he replied.

"Jog it well then. When I'm dropped off—I'm really going to Singapore this time—you'll be taken for what we call a 'physical.'"

"Am I being conscripted?" asked Fury.

Briscoe studied him wistfully. "Personally, I wish that were possible. I mean that, sincerely. You have a certain quality about you that I really like. But I fear that quality would not in the long run serve my best interests. So it is our mutual misfortune that you must be interrogated by fair means and foul, and then scrapped. That's if you're lucky. My silent friend here—" Briscoe patted one shoulder of the elderly Chinese beside him—"knows of some peculiar radiation experiments his comrades are performing on live subjects far north of here. It seems they haven't been able to pit too many round-eyes against native talent in the Mushroom Test Match."

"Land of my dreams, and all the tea I can drink," rued Fury. "What am I to be interrogated for?"

Briscoe chuckled. "You'll be giving us a rundown on what you've done and whom you've seen since coming here. My friend also desires to confirm your true identity. He doesn't know you as well as I do and is eager to make your acquaintance. Had a chat with him this morning and he suspects you're some kind of American secret agent." Briscoe shook his head. "Don't worry, though, it's only a matter of form."

"How did you know I'd come to the office?" asked Fury, noting the approach signs to Kai Tak whizzing past outside.

Briscoe shrugged. "We didn't. But when you vanished last night after dispensing with Carlton, we put some watchers to work. We knew you didn't return to your hotel; in fact, you'd been checked out. We put some people at other places you've been known to frequent, and others all over. Finally, this morning you were seen entering the Wanchai building. We were all so relieved. I booked a later flight to Singapore and made arrangements for your pick-up."

Briscoe wagged a finger. "One thing I *am* curious to know is where you went after dropping Miss Lee off up in the hills. Not a very gallant gesture, by the way."

"Does that matter now?"

"Of course it does, Merritt. You don't strike me as an exemplary student of Dale Carnegie, so we'd like to know whom *you* could be so chummy with that he'd put you up for a night. One of you is quite enough."

They were in the airport now. Briscoe turned around in his seat and checked the contents of his briefcase, examined his tickets, and glanced at his watch. As they coasted to the discharge point, Fury wondered if he was fast enough to jump out, and if not, then cause a commotion trying to. He couldn't see any other alternative.

As they pulled up, the goons at his sides both reached up and drew their window curtains closed. So much for a public spectacle.

Briscoe faced him again when they had come to a stop. "I almost forgot, old friend. There's the question of your estate."

"I name you sole heir?" guessed Fury.

"Yes. One of the things you're going to be giving my friend here *is* samples of your autograph. One sample, expertly applied by you, will go onto a document in which you agree to sell your interest in Bluelist. The others, long after you're beyond any need for them, will be used to transfer your selling price back to Bluelist some time in the future. Don't worry, though: Everything will be perfectly legal and according to form." Briscoe paused and smiled cordially. "Well," he sighed, "it was nice doing business with you, Merritt. I'd shake hands with you now, but I fear that would not be wise. Remember now," he cautioned with a wink of one eye, "think chocolates."

Before Briscoe could pull the partition shut, Fury gritted his teeth as he snatched his briefcase off his lap by the handle, swung it with all his strength to one side and smashed it into the face of the goon on his left, swung it back again at the goon on his right, then leaned forward and swung it at the glass partition. He missed, misjudging the depth of his seat and the roominess of the rear compartment, and before he could push himself back up, something slammed violently on his back so hard that it knocked the wind out of him and pitched him onto the rug, paralyzed. The last time that had happened to him was when he was six and had fallen off some monkey bars flat on his back. All his concentration had been needed then to regain his breath and it was no different now. As he lay gasping for air, his arms were jerked away from his sides, then pinioned behind him, and he heard and felt what he thought were handcuffs being slipped around his wrists. He heard someone say something, a door slam shut, and then the Rolls moved. He braced himself to move again. Then, suddenly, something silver invaded the periphery of his consciousness and a last bolt of pain brought the sky down in his mind.

想念巧克力

Chapter 10

All the
Answers

Consciousness came back to him in bits and pieces, in a swift, rushing jumble of echoing words and sounds and pressures and brief half-images. There was a distinct absence of light, then sudden flashes of it that exploded in front of his face, then right, then left. Finally, something soft hit the front of his body, and the chaos ceased.

It came back with effort. Something dark and comforting and soothingly alien became engaged in a tug-of-war with his half-conscious desire to climb out of the darkness that was caused by the pain in his arms and in the back of his head. The slippery darkness seemed to offer refuge from the pain, and it attacked relentlessly, seeming to soak up his strength and will to fight it. But he knew—knew it very well in that dimension-less, subconscious world—that if and when he could open his eyes, he would have it beaten and under control. The skin around his eyes and even his eyelids felt numb, and he thought he was gritting his teeth as he forced his eyes open with an ef-fort that left him panting and sensitive to stinging rivulets of sweat that rolled off his brow and into his eyes.

He lay still—unconscious now only of time—until all his

battered senses recovered, re-aligned, and re-integrated. Tension came back to his inert muscles, and after a while he could move his eyes. He looked around, all the time fighting to push back that strange, compelling darkness—only a desire now—with its lure of safe, much-needed sleep.

It was a cell, a small cube of stone walls with a weak, dirty bulb hanging like a speckled yellow moon high from a flat ceiling. He was lying face down on a moldy blanket on a canvas cot. He moved his arms and felt his wrists press against cold hardness; the handcuffs still locked his arms behind his back. He curbed his breathing and listened, futilely, in the total silence.

He grew dizzy when he raised his head. He resisted the temptation to let it fall back on the blanket and shook it slowly, painfully, back and forth, and then violently, to clear the numbness from his mind, and to defy the sweet urge to cease movement and lapse into sleep. His arms were two dead weights which ached when he flexed them. Biting into his lower lip, he pressed the heels of his palms together, off and on, off and on, counting to ten and stopping when he felt the cramps coming, then counting again when he thought it safe to repeat the exercise. He stopped only when his limbs felt warm and alive and, in a ragged, sore way, part of him again.

He lifted his head once more and looked around. The walls, probably granite, were pierced regularly all about with little square holes that might have once held fixtures for shelving. The cubicle, perhaps nine by nine, might have once been a storage room, or a pantry.

He strained his neck back and saw the door near the other end of the cot, a heavy metal door of the type found in older American office buildings. There was no knob on it and no clue as to whether it opened in or out, right or left.

He lay his head down again to wait, marking time by flexing his hands open and shut and tensing his legs. There was no point in attempting to stand up, nothing else to see or do. He might need all his strength. He wanted to be found exactly as they had left him, even to the wrinkles on his shirt.

His shirt: He realized that his jacket was gone, as were his tie and belt. He moved his feet together and heard more than felt the far-away "clock" of the soles of his shoes banging together.

Then he heard the faint clink of sound from the door. He closed his eyes and relaxed his body. The "clink" grew into the recognizable sound of a knob being turned, and a slight breeze of air passed over the skin of his face.

He heard two sets of footsteps come inside, then a giggle, followed by an exchange in Chinese. It seemed to be a speculative discussion about him. Something was put down close to the cot, then adjusted as wood scraped over the stone floor. A table, he thought. Metal clattered as someone put something hollow, then something heavy, on top of it. Fury wondered if he should risk opening his eyes, but made himself wait. There was another exchange; one of them seemed to be in doubt. Finally, footsteps clicked away and the door closed emphatically after a last exchange of words.

Cloth rustled as someone reached over and picked up his hand-cuffed wrists. He heard a sigh, then a finger suddenly touched his eyelid and opened it. Fury saw nothing, keeping his sight as blurred and unfocused as possible. Apparently satisfied, the finger disappeared and he felt his hands drop and heard the cloth rustle again. Then his hands were gripped harder by the cuffs and he heard and almost felt the unmistakable rasp of metal as a key was inserted in the lock.

It was all he could do to restrain an urge of hope from shooting up his spine; he had the ridiculous notion that it might be noticed.

One of his hands—the left one—was lifted and brought over to the table, the limp fingers straightened out roughly, then brought down and, one by one, rolled through something soft and wet. Each was then pressed deftly onto some cool, smooth surface.

Fingerprints??

Then his hand was thrown over and it dropped to smack onto the stone floor. There was a pause, a sigh, and the scraping of the table being pushed away. A hand closed on the upper portion of his dangling arm and another took a fistful of his trousers by the hip and together they tried to turn him over.

He wanted to get to the other hand by the wall, thought Fury. His right hand. If he was going to be fingerprinted properly, he must be turned over.

The man heaved again, and then Fury woke up, rolling over to throw him off balance and bringing up his free arm against the man's legs to make sure he fell. The man's forehead cracked against the wall and he fell next to Fury face down. Fury rolled over on top of him as the man tried to push back up, then slapped his hand, black with ink, over the man's mouth as it opened to scream. As he wrapped it around the face, teeth sank into the loose skin between his thumb and index finger. He bore down with his other forearm on the knob of the man's neck as the man's muffled cry blew hotly in his palm, twisted the face up, and stopped when he heard and felt the bone snap.

Fury climbed off the cot and fell against the wall by the door, breathing deeply. He glanced at the body, then at the table. On it were a black ink pad, several white, police-type fingerprint forms—one of which had all the prints of his left hand under a fresh color photograph of himself, all the notations in Chinese—and a gun, a .45 automatic, its safety off, next to the forms. And the key to the handcuffs.

The dead man stared back up at him in a frozen accusation made ludicrous by the smudged ink on his face. His lips were curled in a snarl; black ink and blood smeared his clenched teeth. Fury found himself recalling Annette Hitchings' remark about some contemporary music group; the face reminded him of a concert poster he'd once seen in New York. It belonged to the elderly Chinese who had climbed into the front seat before Briscoe.

Seeing it also triggered an awareness of pain. Fury glanced at his hand; the loose skin, while not severed, was a bloody, shredded mess. He tore a strip from his shirtsleeve, and as he wound it around his hand something that might have been a joke about mad men and rabies fleeted tentatively through his mind.

And on his exposed left wrist he noticed a tiny strip of plastic bandage crossed over one of the veins. He lifted it a bit and saw the red puncture mark. He'd been injected with something, and now the strange, sweaty compulsion to sleep made sense to him. Now that he knew its origin, he could fight it better. The numbness around his eyes had been replaced by a stinging inflammation, and he could feel the press of sleep on the rim of his consciousness. All he had to do was keep it in check, keep it distant, just long enough for him to leave wherever the hell he was.

He finished the knot with his teeth and right hand, then paused and took a deep, conclusive breath. He took the key and removed the other handcuff. The dead man had brought nothing else with which to clean his hands; he wiped them the best he could on the man's jacket, which he then searched. He found a wallet, the contents of which—several laminated identification cards in Chinese, credit cards, some snapshots of some overdone woman, a folded slip of paper with Chinese writing, a wad of Hong Kong money—told him nothing about the man. He put the wallet in his own back pocket; it might be of interest to Amber and her friends—if he ever saw her again.

There was a pack of Japanese cigarettes in the man's shirt

pocket and an engraved Zippo lighter and change in the pants. He tossed the cigarettes aside, and took the form with his photo and prints on it and lit it with the Zippo, dropping the flame to the stone floor when it had burned down to his fingertips.

His last problem was that he still didn't know which way the door opened. Someone was bound to come back for the one on the cot sooner or later—probably sooner; how long could it possibly take to do a man's fingerprints? He examined the door, gun in hand, and noted how the frame covered the door. How stupid of him. Of course; it opened outward, away from him.

Where to wait now? In a corner, near the wall of the door. Someone should be back shortly. Fury chose a corner and waited. The dead man's watch said two-thirty, he remembered. He'd been here—wherever this was—for almost two hours. Or perhaps fourteen. He couldn't know for certain. But they'd taken his picture, his fingerprints, and God only knew what else. Some operation, Harry.

Thinking took his mind off the persistent pain in his bandaged hand. Some operation for a Far East trader. Sir Harold Grampian Briscoe, agent extraordinary. Imports and exports. We Deal In Anything. Could Briscoe have been right about factional clashes within the different British agencies? If so, it would certainly explain Amber. It seemed plausible enough: The traditionalists standing on the status quo and perhaps a shred of morality, versus some activist newer generation of policymakers whose deadly, though perceptive view of the modern world caused them to adopt the most suicidal policies imaginable.

Then he tensed himself at the sound of someone beyond the door. He crouched low and held the .45 out with both hands. Mercifully, the door swung open away from him, so that he would not be noticed in the corner. The man who appeared was the chauffeur with the massive hands. He stepped in and gawked at the sight on the cot. Surprise was on Fury's side completely; the bizarre way the goon's friend stared back up at him froze the other's attention. Fury made an instant decision not to fire the gun or even address the man. Instead, he thumbed the safety on, reversed the gun in his right hand, then stepped forward and pistol-whipped him as hard as he could on the back of the head, almost losing his balance in the act.

The chauffeur pitched forward and fell on top of his friend on the cot. There was a shout from outside. Fury spun around, flicking the safety off. The cell was at the end of a small corridor, along which were several doors. The third goon from Briscoe's limousine was in the corridor, coming with a black bag in one hand and under the other arm some kind of machine. Fury raised the gun and fired, then was out of the cell and past the man as he fell, rushing toward a door out of which a face had peered in surprise at the commotion. Fury gave it his hardest shoulder, stumbling forward as it rocketed open and catapulted the owner of the face to the floor. The man rolled over, reaching inside a white smock and bringing out only the grip of a .45 before Fury fired and hit him in the neck. There was an exclamation to his left: "What in bloody hell *is* this??" Fury turned and found another man in a white smock, who was stretched out over a desk with a gun he'd just retrieved from a coat pocket hanging on the wall; as he swung around with it, Fury fired again and hit the heart, and the man collapsed immediately to the floor.

Fury turned and faced the door and stood stock still to let the ringing thunder fade away from his ears. Soon, all he could hear was the subdued purr of air-conditioning. He strode back to the cell and checked the goon he'd pistol-whipped: dead with a cracked skull. Fury paused longer over the goon in the corridor; in the black bag were syringes and vials of drugs. The machine he identified as a portable lie-detector. He grunted in

surprise; Briscoe *had* been under the impression that he was
some kind of secret agent. A dubious compliment.

Back in the second room, Fury surveyed the ruins. The man
on the floor was a young Chinese, and the one by the desk was
a middle-aged Briton—or at least the "bloody hell" part of
him was. He had been making an inventory of Fury's personal
items; his driver's license, credit cards, and everything else had
been removed from his wallet and laid out neatly over the desk.
In another corner of the room was a stool and a high work-
bench, on which were various microscopes, a row of outsized
brown volumes marked alphabetically, and his passport, a page
of which lay pinched between glass. Next to it, one of the
brown volumes was open to a page on which was reproduced a
blow-up of the Luxembourg business visa stamp. He guessed
that this was where the young Chinese had been working when
the commotion started. At the end of the bench sat his briefcase, locked open but its contents as yet undisturbed.

There were other desks and file cabinets in the room; Fury
tried them but they were all locked.

Across the corridor he found a darkroom, equipped with
enlargers, racks of chemicals and two wash basins. Hung out to
dry on a plastic wire above the basins were several telescopic
photographs of the deck armament of Australian and American warships anchored in Hong Kong Harbour. The drug in
his system was making a fresh assault on his mind and he
stared stupidly at the prints, wondering why their presence
here bothered him. He put the gun down and splashed hand-
fuls of intoxicating, cold water over his face in a basin. As he
dried himself with a towel he studied a shelf containing a vari-
ety of cameras, from the latest Instamatics to a matchbook-
sized Minox.

Back in the laboratory—he could think of no other term for
the room—he reclaimed his property and put his coat back on.
He wondered whether he was in Red China. It was conceiv-

able; the border was only half an hour's drive from the Mandarin through the New Territories.

With gun in hand, he strode down to the other end of the
corridor. Here he found stone steps leading up to a thick
oaken door that had four bolt locks threaded together by a ver-
tical fifth. But to his left was another oaken door with only one
bolt. He eased it away, and, bracing himself against the door in
case it squeaked, pulled on the antique handle and opened it
half an inch. Sunlight poured in—almost blinding him—as
did the sounds of wind in the trees, chirping birds, and an in-
distinct rumble—and distant voices.

He bit into his lower lip as his thumb flicked off the gun's
safety, then he positioned himself at the crack. Squinting, he
could see the ocean far below, the blue sky above, swaying trees
descending down a series of neat garden terraces, and the gray
Rolls parked not two feet away on the gravel.

Beyond the Rolls, soaring far above a cluster of trees, on
a black flagpole, a Union Jack rippled lazily in the breeze.
And below, down on the next terrace, two women were playing tennis.

✳   ✳   ✳   ✳   ✳

Briscoe's house, on Repulse Bay. Fury opened the door an
inch more. Of course. He could see Lamma Island, and beyond
that Lantau Island, twice as big as Hong Kong. There were
junks and sampans in the water, out fishing, and the white sails
of tiny sailboats, and a Star Ferry was heading back from
Lamma in his direction for Victoria Harbour.

Fury leaned back on the stone wall in relief. At least he was-
n't in completely hostile country. He had been a guest here
once, long ago it seemed, at the beginning of Bluelist.

He went back, made a last check of his possessions, then
tucked his briefcase under one arm and slipped out the oaken

door. Outside, unnoticed by the women on the tennis court, he looked into the Rolls; the keys were still in the ignition. He took them; he might have to leave here in a hurry.

Going up the steps that led to the next level, Fury paused to watch the women for a moment. He recognized one of them from last year. Briscoe had invited the new partners of Bluelist here for a celebration; the woman was one of several he had made available as companions. She had ventured a question about his astrological sign. Fury could not now remember what his answer had been, or what had been her name.

The steps led to a patio that was directly above the cellar in which he had been kept. He crossed it and let himself in through the open French doors on the first floor. Briscoe's house, a mansion of Tudor and Norman, hadn't changed. It had only fifteen rooms, but they were big rooms. Briscoe occupied all of downstairs, he remembered, and upstairs was mostly guest rooms and servants' quarters.

The place was more a museum than a residence, and a military museum at that. Antique firearms, swords, knives, helmets, pikes, and lances bristled from the walls of every room. The man had probably spent more on his hobby—one which never showed in his business life—than he could possibly ask for the house on Hong Kong's tight real estate market, one of the dearest in the world.

Fury paused beneath his favorite, one he loved for the sheer esthetic thrill it gave him, an eighteenth century Turkish sword that flowed a gleaming three feet from an almost stylized, modern fleur-de-lis quillon along the gentlest curve of metal he'd ever seen, only a fraction of an inch thick and only an inch wide from the hilt to the tip. The pommel above the grip leaned in contradirection to the tip of the blade and accentuated the curve. It hung horizontally in a walnut panel above the wide stairs that led to the guest rooms. Fury smiled up at it; it was the sole thing of Briscoe's he coveted.

he wondered if the curved knives the Triad boys had
him with yesterday had come from Briscoe's collection. He doubted it. His mind lethargically tried to recall
whose idea the Dying Stars attack was. Pok's or Briscoe's? He
shook his head and moved on.

Oddly enough, there was no one else around. Briscoe's Chinese manservants were not in evidence, though he could hear
the kitchen staff chatting up a storm beneath the muffled clatter of dishes and cookware on the other side of the house. The
muted chimes of the clock in Briscoe's study struck three. One
of the women on the tennis court shouted and laughed.

He mounted the stairs quietly anyway, and walked softly
through the carpeted hall, opening the doors briefly and glancing into each room, searching for Pelosi's. He found it easily
enough. On the nightstand by the made bed was a fold-in family portrait photograph of Pelosi, his wife, and two teenaged
sons. How homey, thought Fury. If only his wife and children
knew what kind of company Walter kept.

In the bathroom, he washed his injured hand again and
dressed it properly from a first-aid kit in the mirror shelf above
the basin. He would have to see a doctor about it—later.

Finished, Fury returned to the bedroom and began searching for something that would link Pelosi to Briscoe. He
thought he found it in a closet. There were three roomy clos-
ets, but Pelosi was using only one. What he found was stashed
behind some luggage, a heavy black leather briefcase very unlike the lightweight gray Samsonite Pelosi had brought to the
meeting at Bluelist two days ago. It had trick catches and a
combination lock and it also needed a key. Fury took down
one of the Oriental knives which decorated the walls. Five
minutes of slitting, slashing and prying with it removed one of
the undersides. The briefcase struck him as odd because it was
unusual for anyone to bring *two* of them all the way from San
Francisco.

He took out a kind of collapsible file. In it were correspondence, memos, sheets of calculations, a currency conversion table, and a pamphlet of U.S. import tariff schedules for ores, all
of it smudged and wrinkled from constant perusal. And it was
all pertinent to what he was looking for, but the most valuable
thing to Fury was the correspondence between Harry Briscoe
and a Washington D.C. law firm by the name of Seton, Corgi,
Pelosi and Norde. There were Briscoe's letters and Pelosi's replies in carbons, the earliest dated three years ago. They all
concerned tungsten, Hong Kong, U.S. demand estimates, the
political climate, and a party referred to only by the name of
"Snapdragon"—probably Briscoe's not-too-subtle code name
for Peking.

Fury lit a cigarette—a blessed Rothman this time—and sat
down on the bed. It was difficult to determine who had started
the exchange. Both men's earliest notes started with the same
"Re our conversation of March 16th at the Brown Palace"—
a hotel in Denver. A quick scan of the letters gave him the picture. Seton, Corgi, Pelosi and Norde, attorneys at law, did
not so much represent clients in court as they did plaintiffs
in Congress and in the myriad agencies and bureaucracies in
Washington. They were a company of professional lobby-
ists—but lobbying for whom? Their correspondence over-
whelmingly pointed to Briscoe and "Snapdragon."

The names of Senators Bookin and Denning, authors of
the tungsten bill, figured largely and often in the letters,
mainly in Pelosi's. They were described by him as "two public-
spirited men of the highest integrity and purest patriotism,
who are seriously concerned about the unrestrained depletion
of this country's vital ore reserves." Bookin and Denning were
subsequently sold on the idea of putting a price ceiling on
tungsten. They had also both been re-elected to their seats in
Congress; in an almost condescending remark Briscoe spoke
warmly of Denning's campaign slogan, "Before America can

look after the rest of the world, she must first look after herself." There was reference to a letter of appreciation from Bookin thanking Briscoe and "Snapdragon" for a contribution—amount not mentioned—to his election organization.

Also at Briscoe's suggestion, and via funds deposited in a San Francisco bank by Snapdragon, Pelosi bought into a financially troubled West Coast toy importer as a silent partner—three months before the founding of Bluelist.

Perhaps the most significant statement he found in the correspondence was Pelosi's assurance to Briscoe that "friends of mine in the State Department have ascertained that U.S. dependency on this commodity on foreign sources would not be frowned upon in certain quarters of the Executive branch. Indeed, conversations with contacts, whose veracity in these matters is above question, suggest that such a situation would not be incompatible with overall foreign policy objectives in the long term, and that it would contribute intrinsically to the establishment of a mutually profitable and tangible stabilization of our foreign relations . . ."

There followed a mild rebuke from Briscoe to Pelosi for discussing the scheme with people who were in or who had access to the State Department, countered with an equally mild expression of satisfaction that at least they knew how well the idea would be received.

More shocking to Fury than the conspiracy to make the United States dependent for an important industrial material on a hostile power, was the extent of Pelosi's refusal to acknowledge just who that power was.

To Fury, there were two classes of evil: conscious, and mindless. The first, one could see and fight because it thrived on recognition. The other was the handmaiden of the first, but almost impossible to fight because when it wasn't running from you, it was running from itself.

Well, this half of the mystery was cleared up, thought Fury, shoving the papers back into the folder. There was probably much more to it, but half an hour's reading had given him the gist of it. He put the file in his own briefcase, then returned Pelosi's to the closet with the luggage. The file was a perfect instrument of blackmail on two counts: he could force Pelosi to kill the tungsten bill; or, failing that, it could serve as an insurance policy for his own life. Of the two, he thought the first alternative the likelier.

Should he wait for Pelosi to come back and then hit him over the head with something? It was what he felt like doing. Then he could throw him out of the window—with a rope around his neck. Fury shook his head again and ground the back of his hand over his brow. Good God, what was he thinking? He had to get out of here. To hell with Pelosi. Pelosi was finished.

He used the phone on the nightstand to call Ronald Tinto and asked him to convey his apologies to the men he was to have seen this afternoon; Would he please set up new appointments at their earliest convenience? He told Tinto nothing about Bluelist or why he had not kept the appointments.

To hell with Pelosi. Fine, he thought, but he was curious about one thing, though, and had a question for the bogus toy dealer: Why had he brought the evidence with him? Fury ran several possible answers over in his mind, then persuaded himself that he'd do better if he slept on it—in the safety of Amber's apartment.

With the briefcase in one hand and the automatic in the other, Fury left Pelosi's room. As he strode through the French doors downstairs and down the patio steps, a car rounded the corner of the house, pulled into the gravel yard and parked beside the Rolls. Fury stopped. It was the Mercedes he'd seen at Cloudy Hill the day before. The driver of the Rolls that had brought him here stepped out, opened the rear door, and out bounced Walter Pelosi, full of good cheer. Things must have been going well for him. Hadn't a trouble in the world. He looked up and froze when he saw Fury. The chauffeur followed his glance, then reached instantly inside his jacket.

Fury raised his gun just in time and fired three times, putting a large red hole in the chauffeur's forehead and another in his gun hand—the first slug smashed a window in the Mercedes. The chauffeur flew back against the car, then fell face down at Pelosi's feet. One of the women on the tennis court screamed.

Fury walked up to Pelosi and considered the man's face. He said, "Snapdragon's dead, Walter. I've got the file, and you've got time to get out of Hong Kong, if you have an open return ticket. Before you're arrested."

"What?" whimpered Pelosi.

Fury shrugged. "I'd love to spend time explaining it all to you, Walter, but I've had enough killing for one day. Excuse me." He glanced inside the Mercedes. Keys in this ignition, too. He pushed the immobile Pelosi aside, slammed the rear door shut, got in, turned the motor over, and drove away.

Glancing in the rear-view mirror, he saw Pelosi in the cloud of gravel dust, still standing, looking down at the dead chauffeur, probably wondering what in hell was happening. He didn't think Pelosi had yet grasped the situation. Well, thought Fury, wait until he starts packing his bags. He shook his head in disgust: The once and never-to-be tungsten tycoon.

所有的答案

Chapter 11

The Stuff
of
Dreams

It ended as it had started, in a dream, a restless, aggressive dream, in which the sounds of reality merged with those in his mind and made it hard for him to distinguish between the two.

He saw himself leaving the Mercedes parked in a street in the Wanchai District, then reclaiming the MGB from the car-park and driving warily, tiredly up the hill to Amber's place. I'll settle with Briscoe tomorrow, he told himself. Then he was in her apartment, and saw that she had not returned. The bed was still unmade. Exhaustion, and the strain of fighting the sleep-inducing drug caught up with him at last, weighing down his aching body and torturing the skin around his eyes with little electric pricks of pain. He shook off his coat and laid the gun on the dresser near Amber's perfume bottles. He kicked the briefcase under the bed, on which he then collapsed, resting a clenched fist on his forehead. Soon the light from her living room faded and his ears picked up the sounds from be-yond the window—the whirl and hum of distant machinery, the constant hammering and pounding of workmen on scaf-folding, car horns, ferry horns, ocean-going horns, church bells,

and clock chimes, the roar of jet aircraft, and a door slammed
shut somewhere in the building. . . . .

. . . I'll just rest for a while, he thought, then I'll make a
good stiff drink and some black coffee and look up some of
those bylines, names he'd seen so often in American and British
newspapers. Give it to the police? No, too big a chance doing
that, too big a risk, they might quash it. . . . Remember Inspector Hung? . . . . No, the best thing to do now was give the
whole thing to some of those journalists. . . . Special to the
Times, Special to the *Journal,* Special—Special—Special. . . .
What to do about Briscoe? And Pok, and Ping? . . . No contract for the able Mr. Rutledge of Matheson and Tuttle now,
they don't know their scheme is shot yet. . . . Should he try and
catch them when they returned? No, what the hell was he
thinking? . . . . The police will pick them up right at the airport, if they ever come back. . . . Even if they're given kid glove
treatment, their scheme is finished. . . . Tomorrow, yes, tomorrow. . . . Good thing the police aren't looking for me. No,
surely they'd have come to the offices by now? And me, I
passed several uniforms in Wanchai and no one looked at me
twice. . . . Hung should have an APB out on me, if they have
APBs here. . . . Well, be glad you've come this far, and you *must*
give Pelosi's papers to somebody, before the police find you,
because they won't want to risk offending Peking, they won't
want to see any of this get out. . . . Wonder if journalists and
papers here are bound by the British Press Law? . . . Blue
Slip? . . . D-Slip? . . . D-Notice? . . . Official Secrets Act? . . .
Must be someone here who'd throw it out the window. . . . . .
Damn all their stupidity, and cowardice, and indifference!
We're at war, but we're not at war. . . . Damn the cowardice!
. . . You know, when I was younger, when I was just a kid in
Wilkes-Barre supporting myself with odd jobs, I never took
God seriously, I objected to the very notion, but I never really
cared whether He existed or not, never gave it a thought, I just

went ahead and did what I wanted, regardless, and if He wanted to make trouble, I was ready for Him, and if I died I much preferred that to living with a threat over my head. . . . . So surely, the least you people can do is . . . . What am I thinking now?? Fine time to slip into theology! How many Briscoes can dance on the head of a pin? . . . .

Amber—Amber suddenly appeared before him, neat and trim, so severe and serious. . . . It was wonderful, loving her, it was the kind of love that suited him. . . . How many times had he observed other people falling in love and then thinking that it gave them the right to give up, to become sloppy and mean and beaten and revolting? . . . What in hell are you thinking of now? . . .

She was saying things to him in his dream. . . . *She's* mixed up in this Briscoe business, he thought, with her gun and her foreknowledge, and he realized that she was always watching him. . . . Watching. . . . Yes, I know all about you, Merritt, all about you. . . . You were perfect for the job, and I was the only one who appreciated that. . . . I know about Tanjeloff and Winch in Buenos Aires, and about that extortionist—Wigand was his name, right?—in Andorra, and how you killed him on his yacht, and I know about Silky McQueen in London, he was a procurer of women for the Arabs, wasn't he? And when he couldn't procure, he kidnapped, and he made the mistake of kidnapping someone close to you. . . . I know all about your arranging that smuggling deal in Hamburg. . . . I know all about your precarious life. . . . The life you led after you left that factory in Long Island City. . . . I know all about your guns and your business deals and you've led a perfectly scandalous life, my love, and you ought to be ashamed of yourself, but you're not, and I love you for that. . . . We knew all there was to know about you months ago, we spent money on agents and bribes to collect everything we could about you, but of what value is intelligence if one cannot draw conclusions from it? . . . The others doubted if you'd bother to come as far as you have, or even make a start, they were terribly surprised, they were all so skeptical. . . . And why not? You are a criminal in the eyes of those whose moral standard is based on degrees of craven submission. . . . But I saw you, knew you, understood you, it was a character judgment, my love, that was the conclusion to be drawn. . . . You've been serving our purposes, and I've been serving you. . . . Love, please forgive me, all I had to do was stand by and watch you almost kill yourself. . . . There was no other way, we who must someday fight for our independence can't show ourselves or interfere in any way, not just yet. . . . I was so afraid you'd die for some stupid reason, it was hell knowing where you were and what was being done to you. . . . I hope you're not angry with us—No! Be angry! You have every right to be, you've been doing our work. . . . Our work. . . . I was so afraid I'd lose you!

Then something sharp and insistent bore into the side of his neck and abruptly dissolved the unreality swimming through his mind, something that seemed to be a part of the careening dream he was having. . . . He let his senses focus on it as it dug deeper and deeper, like a knife, or a stiletto. . . . He had the advantage that they didn't know he knew they were here. . . . Didn't know he was awake and alert. . . . So, he thought, here we go again—

He jerked away from the sharpness and started to roll over, but—

What he found himself doing instead was pushing up with his elbows so suddenly that he startled Amber, who had been resting her head on his chest. She jumped up, her hands flying away.

Instantly he understood what had been digging into his neck: one of her polished nails. "Amber . . . ?" he said in amazement, and then collapsed.

She fell back on him again and kissed him deeply, desperately. That brought him back to reality. After a moment, she relented, and with one last breath into his mouth, held his head in her hands. "Were you having a nightmare, Merritt?" she whispered into his ear.

"No," he managed to say. "I don't think so." She was back in her office clothes, blazer included. He ran his hand down her flank, then reached and felt her thigh beneath the pleated skirt. The gun was there.

She raised her head to look at him. "I haven't had to wear it so often, not until you."

"How long have I been here?" he asked.

She glanced at the clock on the nightstand. "Since at least six, when I came back. It's almost nine now." She paused. "I couldn't wake you. You . . . looked so exhausted."

"I was—still am. I think I was drugged."

"I think you were, too."

"You know everything?"

She shook her head. "Not this time, love. I didn't . . . expect to see you again—so soon."

He grunted. "You know me."

A tear twinkled in her eye. "Yes," she sobbed, throwing herself back down on him and crying into his shoulder, "I know you! I know you!"

He folded his arms around her and held her. Minutes later, she pushed herself back up and whispered, "Merritt, can you forgive me?"

"Forgive you? For what?"

"Don't you understand? Briscoe—Briscoe is—was my superior. But I have had to work against him, while working for him. Don't you understand? I knew he had plans to kidnap you. I had to know that. . . ."

Fury frowned. "You saw it?"

"No," said Amber, "but an associate of mine did. She was co-opted by Briscoe to be a look-out for police. She told me about it."

Fury thought back. "Was she wearing a pantsuit and a big

hat?"

"Yes." Amber's face looked tortured. "But I couldn't lift a finger to help you, Merritt, not without giving it all away, all our work, all our plans, our plan to destroy Briscoe and his organization, the one that is working through us . . ."

"So Harry's working both sides of the fence." Fury shook his head. His mind was still numb. "Amber," he said, "what happened today would have happened without your help. It happened a lot sooner than I expected . . . Look under the bed, Amber, I brought you a present. It's in my briefcase . . . It's the evidence you need to smash Briscoe." He paused. "I think I need a coffee."

"Yes," she laughed, jumping up and slipping into her shoes by the bed. "You have circles under your eyes and your mouth tastes like old tires!"

"But you should see the file."

"We will look it over together, later. I'll fix some coffee."

"Amber," he called to her as she reached the bedroom door. She stopped and turned. "Were you talking to me in my sleep?"

Her face froze fleetingly, then she smiled. "What could *I* have to say in *your* dreams?"

He grinned. "Nothing you should be ashamed of, either."

In the bathroom he showered, then over the sink splashed handful after handful of deliciously cold water in his face, bracing his skin and mind out of the post-sleep grogginess he disliked so much. He dressed in slacks and a shirt, then went into the living room.

He heard Amber still busy in the kitchen. She'd put a silver tray with a pot of coffee, a demitasse cup and saucer, and a little bowl of sweet biscuits on the coffee table. Sitting beside it was his briefcase. He took a sip of coffee, then went to the curved window to wait for her.

What was happening down there now, he wondered. What

internal upheavals were occurring in those cramped office buildings, what hurried conferences had been called in those little gingerbread buildings of Colonial Administration? The gray mountain of tower that was the Bank of China sat squeezed in between newer hotels and office buildings; all of its windows were lit and he thought he could discern shadows moving in some of them.

There were guns going off down there, guns going off all the time, silent guns, whispering guns, guns people never heard but which were deadly and final all the same. Guns like Pelosi's file, and Briscoe's smile, and Amber's . . . and mine . . . .

As he lit a cigarette, a row of lights flickered off in the little gray tower below.

The doorbell rang. Amber came out, peered through the peephole, then opened the door. In strode Inspector Hung, who bowed in deference to Amber, then approached Fury, extending his hand. "We meet again, Mr. Fury," he said. "I trust you have recuperated from your . . . adventure?"

"Yes," answered Fury, shaking the extended hand. "Somewhat. Thank you." He glanced at Amber questioningly.

Amber said, "He is one of us."

"Us?"

"Briscoe's worst enemies."

"The entire Hong Kong police force?"

Hung laughed and shook his head. "No, Mr. Fury. Would that it were so unanimous. No, just a few of us."

"Very few that I can see," Fury smiled, looking at the both of them.

"Please," said Hung genially, waving to the coffee table, "we wish to discuss this with you."

"You've said that before," chuckled Fury.

"This time, not without its scratches, no?"

Fury laughed and sat opposite him and poured their coffees. "Many, many scratches."

Amber left and came back with another tray and a tea service. When the pouring and stirring were done, Fury asked Hung, "Just what exactly is *your* role in all this?"

"An interested party," said Hung after a sip of tea. "Let us just say that I have had the task of ensuring your legal status here during your stay. Things were arranged so that if you were involved in any . . . err . . . public mishaps, I would have been assigned to your case. If any other senior officer had answered your summons on the Dying Stars, the results would have been less than satisfactory for everyone concerned." He paused for another sip. "And—I perform other functions for our superiors here and in London."

Fury looked to Amber, seated next to Hung. She said, "*I* was your case officer."

"Is *anybody* in charge?"

"You will never meet *him*, Mr. Fury," said Hung.

Fury tried one of the biscuits. "So you're official. So was Briscoe."

"You know so?" inquired Hung.

Fury shrugged. "He didn't deny it."

"Please, then, enlighten us, Mr. Fury. We wish to know everything he told you, and everything that happened. From the time you went to Bluelist this afternoon, to the time you stole the Mercedes."

Fury obliged. When he was finished, he asked, "Did you get Pelosi?"

Hung shook his head. "No. By the time our men arrived, he had vanished."

"I recall leaving him holding the bag."

"He left his luggage."

Fury got up and paced. "How is it possible you're both working against Briscoe in this agency—which you've taken great pains not to name, I've noticed—when he's your superior?"

Hung shook his head. "I am as new a recruit as Miss Lee, but Briscoe's directors in London know nothing of me nor of many such others. It was found necessary to compartmentalize. But Briscoe and his associates are on the verge of being—how shall I put it?—disbarred from further legality. All thanks to you, Mr. Fury."

Fury looked thoughtfully from Hung to Amber, then shook his head. "No, Inspector. I can't accept that. All I've done is scare one rotten deadbeat witless and kill a few thugs. Deadbeats and thugs come a dime a dozen. But Briscoes are rare. You could never convince me that what I did this afternoon has destroyed a multi-billion dollar cabal in the making."

"But you *have*," insisted Hung.

"How? I've done nothing so extraordinary that any one of you people couldn't have done it."

"When the police came to Briscoe's house this afternoon, we found your six friends and everything else."

"What he means," said Amber, prompted by Fury's stone-faced incomprehension, "is that the police found *evidence* of Briscoe's treason. And they in turn were obliged to summon the proper officials—our employer. It is the evidence and exposure of the whole thing we were looking for. There is a difference between our finding such things and the police finding them. *We* can be ordered not to act on what we see—or know—but the police cannot. *We* could not even initiate an investigation into Briscoe or anyone else connected with him even for suspicion, not officially. Not only was it so sensitive a task, but Briscoe was one of our own. Many of his superiors were also ours, most of them ignorant of the full context of what they were directing. We have been following the directives of two separate sets of men, Merritt. It has been no easy task. If any one of *us* had done what you have done, to many minds in London *we* would have been regarded as the enemy, as the traitors. And our allies in London would not have been able to lift a finger to help us. Merritt, *you* made the difference; it would not have been possible without you. Can you understand that?"

Fury lit a cigarette, and at length replied, "I think I said something about yours being a twisted profession."

"Twisted by the likes of Briscoe and Pok," said Amber.

"And Pelosi," added Hung.

Fury frowned contemptuously. "Pelosi couldn't twist a pretzel without someone playing seeing-eye dog for him."

Amber picked up the briefcase and took out Pelosi's file. As she began reading through it, Hung went on. "As we were saying, Mr. Fury: Evidence. The man whose neck you broke was the second-in-command of Peking's intelligence apparatus here. His working cover was as a high official with the Bank of China. The man with the large hands and the crushed skull was his personal assistant. In the laboratory, the one dead man was a passport forger—on the Crown payroll, one of ours, yet one of theirs. The other was Elliott Manx, much older than he looked—plastic surgery—in charge of Briscoe's weapons collection, and author of several books on ancient and more recent weapons. One he did on the Thirty Years' War is considered the definitive piece on that period. He was also an active consultant to museums and reputable auction galleries here and in London. We were not sure of him, but he has now been confirmed as having been a static agent. The others?" Hung shrugged. "Card-carrying flunkies."

Fury poured the last of the coffee from the pot. "And what about Briscoe's house? I'd have thought that a man who was running as big and important a scheme as Bluelist wouldn't be allowed to bother himself with comparatively infantile espionage."

Hung said, shaking his head, "Not so. His was one of the most 'safe' houses in Hong Kong, completely above suspicion. It was used, we are beginning to learn, as an intelligence check facility on other espionage activities here. Certain categories of information could be verified there. It also served as a drop for agents who could not risk being seen with or near other Peking agents. Everybody had been warned away from his house until the tungsten scheme was secure—and until you and the others were out of Bluelist."

"What about Pok?" asked Fury. "Surely he wasn't a British agent, too?"

Amber looked up from her reading. "No," she said. "He has been a Peking agent ever since he came here as a refugee twenty years ago. He is actually North Korean. He had the mission of making a success story of himself, subsidized by Peking much the same way Briscoe was subsidized by London."

"And Lon Ping?"

"Lon Ping," mused Hung. "Unfortunately, he is a man we cannot touch—not yet. No matter, though. While his presence in Hong Kong has not yet been publicized, we must leave his future disposition to *his* superiors. We are certain, however, that he must have directed Bluelist for years—or even have conceived of it—for him to risk public association with Briscoe so soon after his arrival. My prediction is that he will need to answer for what has happened now and be recalled before he is made official. No fear, Mr. Fury."

Fury glanced at Amber, who was reading swiftly and intently. "I know you can use it," he said. "How?"

Amber looked up at him and smiled slyly, almost cruelly. "We will keep these—the originals—for our own use. Several copies, under a cover letter from our chief of operations here, will be sent to your F.B.I. These originals will, within a week, be presented to the Prime Minister accompanied by recommendations. Also we will leak portions of the file to the press, to guarantee some action."

Fury took a last sip of coffee. "Presumably, when the news breaks, it will not be news to Briscoe and Pok."

"We are certain they know already," said Hung.

"How will they be dealt with?"

Hung paused, and Fury noticed that Amber had reacted in some minute way to his question. "That is up to them," said the inspector. "They can, as the policeman often says, come along peacefully, or incur drastic consequences. They must understand that there will be no retirement for them in China."

Close to one o'clock in the morning, Hung rose to depart, Pelosi's file under his arm. He advised Fury not to leave Hong Kong for a few days. "You may return to your hotel. Your suite is still reserved. Please send the entire bill to me; it will be taken care of." Fury assured him that his business appointments would keep him in the Colony for at least another week. Hung shook his hand with feeling once more, and was gone.

Fury sat down again, and was so immersed in his thoughts that he did not notice Amber clearing the coffee table. He looked up only when the lights suddenly dimmed. She stood by the open bedroom door, slowly undoing the buttons of her blouse. "It has been a long day for the both of us," she said. "Come to bed."

Minutes later, before he fell asleep in Amber's arms, he said, "It was a great battle, Amber."

砌成夢的種種

Chapter 12

Market
Rally

The *Commodities Quotation* of October 25th carried this item on page two, under the heading, "Tungsten Jumps Charged to PRC Moves; Link Seen with Pending Senate Ceiling Bill":

> Unsubstantiated rumors are circulating in Tokyo and Hong Kong among metals dealers that a syndicate of British banks and Far Eastern trading companies is moving into position to corner the world tungsten market via an exclusive commercial agreement with the People's Republic of China, which has the largest unexploited reserves in the world. Sources have named a Hong Kong-based company, Bluelist Tungsten Trading Co., and a London-based banking consortium represented in Hong Kong by Felicity Bank, as being the principals.
>
> Metals experts and traders say that, if true, the PRC could come to not only dominate tungsten production and marketing, but also wield considerable political and economic influence in much Western, and

in particular, U.S., specialty steel production.

Other knowledgeable sources assert that the rumor could be an illogical reaction to the recent recommendations of a U.S. Senate committee study that U.S. production of tungsten ore be curtailed and the U.S. market thrown open to foreign ore producers.

Neither Bluelist nor Felicity Bank officials were available for comment on the rumors. Senators Bookin and Denning, authors of a bill introduced in the American senate that would implement the report's recommendations, could not be reached for comment.

Fury, in the Marquee restaurant for breakfast near the Mandarin, smiled at the article after a sip of coffee. Delivery promised, delivery made. The same news had also appeared almost verbatim in the *South China Morning Post.* He folded the papers up neatly, put them in his briefcase, and finished his breakfast. He felt energetic despite his lingering exhaustion, and was in high spirits despite the fact that when he woke this morning Amber was gone again, having left another of her notes in a teacup in the kitchen: "No breakfast together this morning. Hung called. Have gone to terminate Briscoe & Co. You *don't* have to go back to the hotel! Be sure to read the papers. This evening, then. Love, Amber." Fury sighed contentedly, paid his bill and left a bigger tip than was called for, and went about his business, so ordered by Amber Lee.

That evening, after an unusually productive day, he had dinner with Paul Chan, the enthusiastic president of Rapid Technologies of New Kowloon, at *La Lumière,* to celebrate their contract for ten thousand basic memory units, January delivery, with an option for fifty thousand in various lots over the next year. He almost laughed at himself as he hurried back close to eleven o'clock, eager to see Amber. But when he let himself into her apartment and stepped into its darkness, he sighed audibly in aching disappointment. Damn it, what was she up to now? Perhaps Briscoe *was* back, he thought, and there had been another call to arms.

He was washing dishes when the doorbell rang. He rushed to the door and opened it. It was Inspector Hung, who, after introducing his companion, Mr. Middlemay, sat aside from them and observed silently.

Mr. Middlemay was a short, trim, engaging man in his healthy sixties and an impeccable, razor-creased pinstriped suit. He took a seat, lay his attache case on the coffee table in front of him, and glanced once at Hung before speaking. Fury caught the officer's eye, too. "Direct from London," said Hung.

"I'll come directly to the point, Mr. Fury," opened Mr. Middlemay in a soft voice trained by decades of deadly White-hall courtesy. "First, it may please you to learn that your actions have precipitated the abrupt resignations of several key persons in the ministries concerned—and at least one attempted suicide. There has been talk of forcing a vote of confidence in the Commons for the Party presently in office, though I must add that the project recently very much in dispute was the brainchild of another diminished, though still formidable, Party. Quite a tempest you've stirred up, Mr. Fury," smiled the gentleman.

"Yes?" said Fury, sitting forward with his wrists on his knees, his hands folded.

Mr. Middlemay continued, unsure of Fury's response. "One thing is certain: the Party in question will most likely need to reshuffle its administrative and Cabinet appointments if it does survive a vote. There's simply no avoiding it. In any case, what has happened has practically blown its chances for retaining its rather thin majority in the Commons. Half a dozen coalitions are brewing for break-up. By-elections are coming up soon, you know. I should have some satisfaction in that, at least."

Fury tattooed his thumbs together.

Mr. Middlemay smiled in understanding. "Here's a bit of information that hasn't made the papers yet: Walter Pelosi attempted suicide—and succeeded. He shot himself some time today after being visited by F.B.I. gentlemen."

Fury spoke. "I'd have been more surprised if he hadn't." He turned to Hung. "Was Briscoe right about Ushio?"

Hung nodded. "He was found where Briscoe said he would be."

Fury remarked, "I must remember to send his company a card." Then he scrutinized Middlemay academically for a moment, and asked, "Why weren't Briscoe and his project dealt with long before this, Mr. Middlemay?"

Mr. Middlemay did little to conceal his distaste for Fury's interrogatory tone. "Because they had friends, Mr. Fury," he answered with sarcastic condescension, "friends with power and influence, friends who never really left government during all the subsequent Governments. And Briscoe's wasn't the only active project of this nature."

"Such as?"

"It's not my privilege to say, Mr. Fury."

"I see," said Fury. "Friends, enemies, and musical chairs. I don't see why you bothered, Mr. Middlemay."

"Excuse me?"

"Wouldn't it have been simpler just to expose all the nonsense, fire everybody concerned, bring up charges of treason, and wipe the slate clean? It would have saved much money and not a few invaluable lives."

Mr. Middlemay went red and drew a sharp breath through his nose in a classic huff. "It can't ever be that *simple*, Mr. Fury. I'll just say that in addition to being somewhat inexpedient, a mass firing such as you suggest might have encouraged a mass defection to the Soviets or to Peking. Furthermore, we have had to tolerate these people—who, we admit, went too far and exceeded their tangent responsibilities—because, well, because we'd rather have them working for *us* than for anyone else."

Fury glanced at Hung, who shook his head and grinned with incredulity. Fury said to Middlemay, "You're selling Peking advanced jet engines and Moscow the next stage of mainframe computers, neither of which has even been used in Britain yet. Honestly, Mr. Middlemay, I don't think either of those countries would place much value on a few out-of-date spysters who, at the present rate, wouldn't even have a chance to steal for them."

"*I* honestly don't see the *connection*, Mr. Fury," said Middlemay.

"And I honestly don't know why you're taking up my time."

With obviously strained self-control, Mr. Middlemay resisted response. "On the matter of Bluelist," he said instead, his voice sliding back into his businesslike tone, "I'm afraid *that* can't continue. Bluelist was a creature of government and must now be dismantled. Sir Briscoe's and See Pok's interests in it have been seized, though because you are the sole meaningful survivor of Bluelist, your interests will be protected. I would advise you to form a new association, if you wish. What I need from you," he said, unlocking his attache case and extracting some forms, "is your signature under an agreement to sell your interest to an authorized representative of the Crown, namely myself. Under the same authorization, I may negotiate a sale price above the value of your original investment," he added, producing a fountain pen, "which I shall enter on the forms above our signatures. Have you a particular figure in mind, Mr. Fury?"

Fury drew one of the forms over and glanced through all the fine print. After a moment he mentioned a figure that was nearly double the value of his interest in Bluelist.

Mr. Middlemay expressed genuine surprise. "I must say, that's far below what we had expected."

Fury adopted his own business tone. "The value added to the base figure represents a bill for services not rendered, Mr. Middlemay. I sold some typewriters to a dealer in Liverpool some years ago. The vessel I sent them on was tied up for weeks by a port workers' strike—that is, by fellow civil servants of yours. The added value represents the demurrage costs —against which there was no insurance—and my British import taxes on that shipment. A quarter of the typewriters were stolen from the warehouse, and the dealer went bankrupt before he could pay me. In sum, the added value represents my costs and my theoretical profit." Then he took a pen and bent to sign the dotted line.

Mr. Middlemay slipped the forms back into his attache case. "You have a most peculiar species of gratitude," he snapped softly. "I should stuff it and put it on exhibit with all the other extinct forms of life, for that, I'm not displeased to say, is what it is fated to be." Middlemay reached into the breast pocket of his coat and whipped a blue card onto the table. "Present *that* to the manager of the Imperial Canadian Bank here any day after tomorrow. He will be expecting you and will arrange to transfer our agreed-upon sum to any bank of your choice."

With that out of his system, Middlemay rose and strode to the door. His hand on the latch, he turned to Fury again. "I want you to know that meeting you has been the most disagreeable duty I have ever had to perform in my career! I'll wait for you downstairs, Inspector." He braced his shoulders, opened the door, and slammed it violently shut after himself.

Fury glanced at Hung, who burst out laughing. Fury chuckled and said with a smile, "You could have warned me." He went to the sideboard. "Have a drink?"

Hung shook his head. "I should have warned *him!*"

"Was he necessary?"

"They wanted to advise you, appraise you, sign you out of the affair."

"It's hard to believe he's on your side."

"You were lucky," chuckled Hung. "He is what is referred to as a 'moderate.'"

Fury brought his drink back to the couch. "Were you waiting for me long?"

"No. He flew in just over an hour ago and reported to Administration. We were informed of your arrival here."

Fury twirled his glass between his palms. "But not by Amber?"

The inspector averted Fury's insistent gaze, and finished his cigarette. "She was in Singapore," he said at last.

"Was?"

"She has returned."

"After Briscoe?"

"We know that he has returned. Smoking him out of hiding will be a delicate task."

"Dangerous?"

"Not particularly." Hung paused. "It cannot be avoided. She is the only one Briscoe trusts now. It was she who convinced him to come back to Hong Kong. And Pok. They believe she is preparing their escape to the north. Through Macao."

Fury was quiet for a moment. "How long will it take?"

Hung shrugged. "Now that he is back—perhaps an hour, perhaps days. He is being very cautious, naturally. He knows that everything is finished for him. And, he is desperate. He cannot even write a check for funds. He has a nest of gold somewhere in the Colony. He will squander it now."

Fury set his glass down hard on the table. "I want in on the kill, Inspector."

Hung shook his head. "You have done enough, Mr. Fury."

"I don't like not finishing what I start."

"A commendable virtue, Mr. Fury. But do not presume there will be a killing. We want very much to have him and Pok alive and undamaged."

Fury rose and took two short steps closer to Hung, studied the watchful officer for a second, then turned and dug his hands in his pockets. He paced a while in front of Hung, then sat suddenly on the edge of the coffee table and leaned toward Hung menacingly. "Tell me the truth, Inspector," he said. "Is there even the slightest possibility that Briscoe may suspect her?"

Hung shook his head. "He trusts her implicitly."

"Why *shouldn't* he suspect her of being on the wrong side?"

"He thinks her a fool, as he thought you a fool. And so many others."

"And Pok?"

"He does not concern himself with these matters. Briscoe is his sole source of information, except for his contacts in the Bank of China."

Fury's gaze bore into Hung. "Are you in contact with her?"

"She may communicate with us, but not we with her. It is too risky."

"Do you know where she is? Now, this moment?"

Hung shook his head again. "I would not tell you even if I knew, Mr. Fury." As gently as he could, he extracted a cigarette from his pack, then offered Fury one. Fury shook his head. He lit up, exhaled once, then said, "You will please pardon me if I perhaps intrude upon forbidden ground, Mr. Fury, but I know, from much the same vantage point, that what you are suffering now is what she suffered after she learned of your kidnapping."

Fury's eyes seemed to grow harder. "You are intruding, Inspector," he said. "Suffering is not in my book of virtues." Then his features softened; he added, "But the intelligence is appreciated."

"How unique," remarked Hung.

"What?"

"That someone should harbor such a sentiment. I find it appealing."

Fury picked up his glass and went to the sideboard again. Pouring his drink, he said, almost casually, "I'm going to marry that woman."

"How curious," said Hung, smiling.

"What?"

"In the strictest confidence, she expressed a similar desire in regards to yourself, Mr. Fury."

⁂   ⁂   ⁂   ⁂   ⁂

The news, plentiful though it was during the next two days, gave him no information about Amber.

Felicity Bank collapsed. Rumors that it was connected with Peking and a simmering scandal caused enough of its regular and commercial depositors to run on it. Bank management ran out of cash and could not call in enough loans to float that shortage. Depositors were quickly followed by bond holders and other creditors, only a small fraction of whom were fortunate enough to recoup a pitiful two cents on the dollar.

Several directors of the Bank of China, Hong Kong, were abruptly called home, for "policy review," as the papers reported. Some authoritative Hong Kong bankers speculated privately in their clubrooms that the collapse of Felicity Bank probably cost the Bank of China somewhere in the neighborhood of three hundred million dollars, and the responsible directors—now on their way back to Peking—their creature comforts, but more likely their lives. There existed professional wonderment at the amount, and there was also wonderment about why the other major principal of Felicity, the Houghton-Devane Group, did not step forward with the necessary credits to cover its affiliate's sudden debts. After all, Houghton-Devane represented some terribly important names in British and international banking, to whom three hundred million was but a trifle, and then there were all those private bond brokers and securities houses threading from the City to the Paris Bourse to Frankfurt to Wall Street. God, the shambles! exclaimed the clubmen over their sherry and gin. What a bubble! They can sweep it under the rug for a while, but it's got to be shaken out sooner or later!

While in New York, in the noisy, clamorous bond room of a brokerage house high above Wall Street, an account manager shouted hoarsely into the receiver of a phone to the firm's broker on the floor of the bond room of the Stock Exchange, "Goddamn it, Hal, get rid of the damned things! Now! . . . *No, now!* Pelosi's executor wants to dump the *whole* portfolio, *now,* for whatever we can get for it! . . . Hal! No—*No,* goddamnit, he doesn't want to swap! Whadaya mean they wanna swap *back??* Who the hell ever heard of swapping *back??* Well, that's their tough cookies!! . . . *What??* Another four points!! . . . Yeah, it just went by on the board up here! Hal, you get your fat behind moving and sell!! Please God sell them or I'm gonna hafta go on food stamps, and *your* commission's shot to hell, too!! . . . Sell, sell, sell!! . . . Hal, can't you get everybody down there who's got China Blue Holdings together and *do* something?? . . . *What?? They're gonna suspend trading?!?!* Hal, hurry and do something before they announce it, dump 'em for *anything* or we're finished! . . . Who's this? . . . Clerk, where's Hal?? Put Hal back on! . . . What's *happening* down there?? . . ."

Editorials appeared in various Far Eastern newspapers citing the value of a central, autonomous government banking system that could at least cushion, if not actually prevent, the possibility of bank failures like that of Felicity in Hong Kong, which had no central bank. Hong Kong editorials, for the most part, countered these attacks on the Colony's banking practices vigorously. "We do not believe," said one, "that forcing the thriftier and wiser to subsidize the errors in judgment—indeed, the outright conspiracy to defraud, as the facts behind the Felicity debacle would seem to indicate—by others, however innocent or guilty, of whatever magnitude, will ensure anyone's prosperity. There is justice to be found in economics, and it is justice which central banking systems, by their very nature and intent of purpose, seek to avoid at all costs, usually at the price of dwindling civil freedoms."

On Friday, Han-su Realty, one of the biggest real estate developers in Hong Kong, declared bankruptcy. It was reported that Han-su, which owned undeveloped tracts in the New Territories and on Lantau Island, and which built a vast block of resettlement towers in New Kowloon under special contract with the housing authorities, was a major creditor of Felicity Bank's. Mr. Tuan Han-su had been a left-wing agitator in his youth, but seemed to have lost his ardor for chanting and banner-waving when he inherited his father's substantial property interests. He then slugged his way up with spectacular real estate ventures in the Colony and in Singapore, joined the ranks of Hong Kong's many opulent millionaires, and earned the local acclaim of the socially concerned and the questionable accolade of "The People's Landlord." Bankers and realty men had expected the Bank of China, with whom Mr. Han-su was known to be intimately associated, to come to his aid. It did not. Mr. Han-su vanished without a trace, never to be heard from again, and the court ordered Han-su Realty into receivership.

Friday evening was to have seen the first formal, though unpublicized, reception for Lon Ping, envoy extraordinary for the People's Republic of China, at Shelbourne House, former palatial residence of Sir Gatwick Weslley-Shelbourne, O.B.E., M.P., veteran of the Burma Road, long deceased, on Deep Water Bay. Shelbourne House had reverted to the National Trust in far-away London, but by special arrangement had been leased in perpetuity to the diplomatic offices of the People's Republic. The reception was cancelled without explanation.

Friday also saw Fury win three more contracts, and Saturday morning's papers brought the news that the Houghton-Devane Group was to become the subject of a special Royal Committee of Inquiry into the government's financial activities abroad, to be seated at the vigorous, forceful behest of both the Shadow Exchequer and the Shadow Minister of Foreign Affairs.

Before the announcement of the investigation, the British home press had played ignorant; Hong Kong and spies had become *passé* copy, so where was the copy in an even duller story concerning an anonymous banking syndicate and the failure of a third-rate affiliate? But there were certain bureau chiefs in the London financial papers who received high-strung story queries from their Far Eastern correspondents and stringers; these chiefs cautiously signalled their replies to come ahead with all there was to know, their individual hunches staying their hands and the guarantees of splashy, front page bylined stories. They collected what was sent, had it written up and then slotted. Soon their taut patience was rewarded with the Royal Committee announcement. Neither the bureau chiefs nor any decent financial editor needed to be told about Regency Road Bank; it was an open but not-much-discussed secret, a subject until now completely devoid of a worthy newspeg. And they hurried; the mass rush to print in Extras was not so much a competition between the papers over who would break the story first as it was a need to beat the whimsical strictures of the Press Secrecy Law.

That morning Fury spread all his contracts out on the coffee table and tabulated their prospective values and his commissions. He would come out far ahead even if one or two of the deals fell through. Tinto had excelled himself this trip; it had been almost love at first sight with every manufacturer the broker had arranged for him to see. Everything he'd come to do was done. And a little more.

Virtually the only problems he encountered were the questions of a new bank account and a new firm. The bank account was easily solved with the presentation of Mr. Middlemay's blue card at the Canadian bank and with the subsequent transfer of the money it represented to another, more commercial bank. Then, on Friday, he instituted the paperwork to incorporate a new import company in Hong Kong, which wouldn't be registered and finalized until the middle of the next week. It would be ready to receive the chocolate shipment long before the bars docked; his second week would be taken up in a search for the right factoring and marketing firms to sell the bars. Derek was due back next week, and he would ask him to recommend someone to manage the new firm.

Tinto had asked him on Thursday, "What the devil is going on with Bluelist, Merritt? I called this morning to settle some messy accounts but someone switched me over and a distinctly Whitehall voice informed me that any inquiries should be directed to a Trade Council office I'd never even heard of."

"There was a disagreement," answered Fury. "The partnership has been dissolved."

Tinto mulled over this answer for a moment. "But—so abruptly?"

"It was the cork in the Felicity bottle," said Fury. "Somebody pulled it."

Around noontime Friday he was finished. Gathering together all the documents and slipping them into his briefcase, he considered how to spend the rest of the afternoon. If he stayed here, in her apartment, he would start listening to her records—she had a fine collection of classical albums—and only wind up pining for her, then growing angry. So he donned slacks and a sports jacket to stroll down the hill to

Central Hong Kong. He forced himself not to think of Amber. No one had contacted him since Hung's visit with Middlemay. And he supposed that he had been watched and followed all this time by people in her organization. Normally, it would have made him uneasy; now, it didn't matter. Again, in a way, he was glad; it was his only form of contact with her.

As he was slipping into his jacket, somebody did contact him. Her phone rang. He answered. It was a call from the American Consulate. They wondered if he could stop by sometime today. Nothing important. Just a passport snag.

Suspecting something a little more serious than that, he went to the consulate, and was met by a consular officer who introduced him to Roger Emrick, of the Federal Bureau of Investigation. Mr. Emrick escorted him to a vacant office. "You're not at all like he described you, Mr. Fury," said Emrick as they took their seats.

"Who?" asked Fury.

"Walter Pelosi. He as much as said you were God's conception of Satan's twin brother. He called you other things, but I won't repeat them. Claimed you rough-housed him and beat him up. We didn't notice any abuse on him, though."

"I suppose he was still upset with me."

Emrick chuckled. "He said you shot someone not two feet away from him."

"His chauffeur, who was going to shoot me."

"Can't blame you for that. Probably would've done the same myself. Want to tell me about it?"

Fury told him about the kidnapping.

When he was finished, Emrick sat quietly for a moment, then said, "You don't believe in negotiation, do you?"

Fury smiled. "Is that all you wanted to know, Mr. Emrick?"

"No, not at all. I'm here to ask you where the rest of Mr. Pelosi's correspondence is."

"What I took from him I gave to the authorities here. I had

no other use for it than to see it cause what's happening."

"Why didn't you hand it over to us?"

Fury shrugged. "This is Hong Kong, and the mess is British." Fury paused. "You're way out of your jurisdiction, Mr. Emrick."

"Yes. Well, I'm on the team that's looking into Pelosi's firm and the activities of a couple of senators. Your name was in what little the Brits gave us."

"How did you find me?"

"I didn't. I called the Mandarin—which is where the consulate here says you usually stay—and somebody at the consulate called you for us." He smiled. "Hear about Pelosi?"

"He killed himself," said Fury. "A pity."

"I'll say it was. We weren't through talking with him. Well, he was nothing but what birds use to soil people's clothes, anyway."

Fury began to take a liking to Mr. Emrick. "Did you have a chance to ask him why he had that file with him?"

"No, we didn't, but we gather from the rest of his law partners that they didn't fully trust this mysterious Mr. Sir Harry Briscoe. They liked what he had to offer but were still leery of him. They wanted to be able to hold something over him if he tried any funny business. We subpoenaed most of their files and found a duplicate of what we were sent by the Brits, plus a lot more. Pretty juicy stuff."

"Can you do anything with it?"

Emrick laughed. "Do anything with it? With what little we have, our principal charge will be conspiracy with a foreign government to suborn Congress. The rest is gravy. We're thinking of holding a blindfold drawing to decide the other charges. Denning even sponsored one of the Acts we'll be charging him with violation of." He laughed again. "He and Bookin are just about finished. There's a move in the Senate to have them censured." He paused. "You're sure there's nothing outstanding we should see, Mr. Fury?"

"I wish there was, Mr. Emrick."

"Of course, you know that when you get back stateside we'll be asking you to testify and otherwise talk a lot."

"You can count on me."

Emrick regarded Fury for a moment. "You know, we got wind, too, that this tungsten bill they had ready would have sailed through the Senate and probably walked through the House with a few riders. There seemed to have been enough votes lined up to override a White House veto. Once it became law, you could have made a bundle and nobody could've touched you. What made you take a knife to it?"

"Maybe I believe in a free country, Mr. Emrick," said Fury. "One in which I don't need the assistance of venal Congressmen to make a fortune."

Emrick shook his head. "Patriotism doesn't suit you. It's the last thing I think of when I look at you. Want to tell me the truth?"

Fury smiled at the man. "Want me to testify for the Attorney General?"

Emrick said nothing. "Well, I guess that's all I wanted to see you about, Mr. Fury. About that file."

Fury stood up. "I'm sorry you have to go back empty-handed. Glad to be of help." He went to the door.

"Hey, Mr. Fury," said Emrick from the desk. Fury turned. "Keep up the good work."

Walking back from the consulate, he came upon a jeweler's shop in Wanchai. The glittering diamond rings in the window winked back at him, daring him to be so fanciful. The fancy grew into a desire to anchor the reality of Amber. He stepped in.

Passing Connaught Centre on his way to the Mandarin for lunch, he heard the sudden skirl of massed bagpipes and the unmistakable staccato of British military drumming. He crossed the street and stood on the outskirts of the crowd. The bands of the resident Indian Gurkha Brigade and the visiting Black Watch were giving an afternoon concert and tattoo. He liked Scottish marching tunes best; they made his adrenalin boil with defiance. And he liked Scottish military tradition. In past wars, the Scots were usually ordered up first to break an enemy's first and strongest line of defense; they invariably suffered the highest casualties. Wits said that this was done because only the Scots were stupid enough to make frontal assaults. Not necessarily, mused Fury.

Somebody tapped him on the elbow. He turned casually, supposing someone wanted to squeeze up front for a better view of the drilling bands. A young Chinese man smiled at him. "Mr. Fury?"

"Yes?"

The man handed him a little, pearl-gray envelope, turned, and walked away without further word.

Fury looked at the envelope, which had no markings, then moved away from the crowd and tore it open. Inside was an embossed white card with flowing script:

> *You are cordially invited to an evening*
> *of graceful idleness and tasteful*
> *decadence at the residence of*
> *Sir John & Lady Satchell,*
> *18 Threadneedle Vista,*
> *Repulse Bay, at 7:30.*
> *Black Tie*
> *Present this card at the door.*

On a slip of paper clipped to the invitation was a handwritten note: "One last ruse, darling. See you there tonight. Amber."

Threadneedle Vista: Briscoe's house was number 16. Welcome to Society. Can you play pin-the-tail? Yes, but no blindfold, thank you.

Chapter 13

Crashing the Party

As he passed it, Briscoe's house, a squat stone mass of Tudor and Norman features, stood dark and silent like a property that had been up for sale for too long. By contrast, the house further up the narrow, winding road was brilliantly lit and already milling with guests enjoying the pleasant, almost windless night air. Fury turned the wheel and pulled the MGB over to the end of a long string of cars parked on the side. He swung out and gave his tux one last brush.

From the road, Satchell House was a wide, expansive mixture of traditional Japanese and California Mission architectural styles resting on and overlapping a much smaller stone foundation. Underneath the jutting first floor on the slope side was a patio that melted into the first of many descending terraces. Esthetically, the house was an abomination; the straight, delicate Japanese lines dominated, but were rendered superfluous by the Mission arches and stone pillars. He wondered what could have possessed the architect's mind when he tacked those on. Perhaps drink.

At a pair of teakwood doors, a servant took his card, then

glanced up at him, trying to place his face. "Your name, sir?"

"Merritt Fury."

"Ah, yes," said the servant, almost with apology, and stepped inside. "Sir John is expecting you. Major Haskins will escort you."

The place seemed designed for parties; large and numerous parties, too, he guessed, his eye roving over the number of people. A series of panels had been rolled in to accommodate a small orchestra, a dance floor, tables, a ring of buffets, and a bar. Waiters and maids circulated constantly with trays of cocktails. The string section of the orchestra was playing café Viennese, and there were couples on the floor doing abbreviated waltzes. The gathering had a charm and ambience he didn't think had survived the last war. He estimated, from beside a potted palm, that roughly half the guests were older people, about one quarter were affluent middle-aged, and the rest were in his age bracket. A number of the men wore military ribbons on their jackets. Everybody looked at home and seemed to be having a good time. Amber was nowhere in sight.

"You *still* have the advantage of me, sir."

Fury turned in surprise and found the irritable Mr. Menzies of Monday morning beaming at him. "Yes," he answered. "I never had a friend at Felicity Bank."

Menzies chuckled. "You know, you're a very hard man to get to know."

Fury glanced at the glass in the man's hand. Obviously it wasn't his first. "Some people regret the effort."

"Well," laughed Menzies, "never mind! Any friend of old Satchy's is a friend of mine! How long have you known him? You can't go back very far."

"I've never met him," said Fury.

"Oh," mused Menzies. "We're old friends, you know. Got pulled off Dunkirk together way back when. Then I went to Birmingham to service Spitfires and Satchy went to a

Maidenhead crypto section. Wasn't that a rotten show?"

"The war? I missed it, I'm afraid."

"No, no, my good fellow. Felicity! I'm glad we only just signed on with them! Still, it was farewell to five thousand pounds."

"Did you inquire about Chan Ha Tze?"

"Yes, we did—you *were* listening in, weren't you?—but some frozen-faced public affairs fish said he'd embezzled funds to pay off some bully boys. We didn't even bother trying to withdraw our account, we would have been penalized half the amount. Then we go and lose the whole lot!" Mr. Menzies frowned lopsidedly.

Fury shrugged. "Commercial banks are for business, savings banks are for certain people."

"Eh?"

"Bad advertising copy," grinned Fury.

"What *do* you do, whatever your name is? You have the oddest sense of humor—"

"Mr. Fury?" interposed another voice. They both turned. The speaker was a trim, fortyish man with military ribbons on his jacket. "Major Haskins," he smiled, nodding to both of them and offering his hand to Fury. As they shook, he said, "Your hosts are eager to make your acquaintance."

Fury nodded cordially to Menzies, and accompanied the officer. "Amber Lee," probed Fury. "She *is* here, isn't she?"

"Why, yes," answered the officer brightly. "She's with Sir John now. Do you know him well?"

"Not at all."

"That's strange. He usually doesn't invite anyone outside his circle."

"Surreptitious invitation," remarked Fury.

"What *do* you do? I suppose you're in some business or other."

"Export-import—"

Halfway across the floor someone caught Fury's arm and exclaimed, "Merritt! This *is* a pleasant surprise!"

Fury stopped and smiled helplessly at the vivacious Annette Hitchings. "Miss Hitchings," he said, nodding to the group of women with her.

"Amber said you'd be here," she purred, taking him aside, "though why you didn't arrive together is beyond me."

"We didn't want to start rumors," replied Fury. "How's Derek?"

"Fine, just fine. He's been following this thing with Bluelist from Sydney and is just dying to ask you a million questions. He'll be back Tuesday or Wednesday. Doesn't he cut quite a figure, Major?"

"Marvelous, I'm sure," said the officer woodenly. "And I see you're your usual self."

"Don't be jealous, Major," smiled Miss Hitchings. "I'm afraid Mr. Fury is already spoken for." She looked away from the officer's red face. "Merritt, you must promise me a dance."

"Of course," said Fury. "What happened to that lunch?"

"I couldn't get in touch with you the whole week—Oh!" she exclaimed again, noticing his bandaged hand and holding it in both of hers. "What did you do to it?"

"A . . . dog bit me," said Fury. "A running dog."

"And what happened to *it?*"

"It rolled over and played dead."

"Goodness, Merritt. Are you rabid?"

"It depends on who is biting."

"Well," she purred playfully again, running a finger down one of his lapels, "you must guarantee that dance. It may be the only time I get to lay a hand on you."

Major Haskins sighed audibly. Miss Hitchings glanced at him. "Why, Morris, don't frown like that. You'd think I'd interrupted your marching Mr. Fury to an execution you were throwing. Dismissed!" she laughed, flicking a hand, then winking at Fury.

As they walked away, Major Haskins glanced back once, then remarked in a low tone, "The dog you killed wouldn't happen to have been a bitch, would it, Mr. Fury?"

"No," answered Fury too smoothly. "It was an overly in-quisitive gelding."

Major Haskins, saying no more, threaded them effortlessly through the crowd to a pair of mahogany doors. As he opened them for Fury, the orchestra began another waltz.

It was a study, a quiet study, and even with the door open, so thoroughly sound-proofed by the thick Persian rug and by the thousands of books on the four walls, that the music and party din behind Fury diminished in volume by half. On one wall was a portrait of the Queen, on another one of Churchill. The room was softly lit by strategically placed table lamps.

Behind an executive oak desk sat a gentleman, and in a red leather armchair was Amber. The gentleman was tall, thin, white-haired, and had a small beard, one of the few Fury had seen on Westerners in Hong Kong. His gray eyes studied him with an interest divided between cold assessment and restrained amazement. Amber was in black again, this time a formal gown, no provocative slit. But it was backless, and her elbow-length black gloves accentuated the bareness of her shoulders. And again her hair was piled, this time falling back so that it framed her face and stressed the grace of her neck. She wore gold earrings, a miniature watch, and no other orna-ment.

She rose when he walked in, but the gentleman remained seated. "Thank you, Major, for spotting Mr. Fury before the society hounds had a chance to ask him embarrassing ques-tions," he said with an odd evenness.

Fury heard the door close gently behind him, and the music and voices shrank to a vague undercurrent. Amber smiled and said, "Merritt, this is Sir John Satchell, my godfather and a very close friend of my parents. Uncle John, this is Merritt Fury."

The gentleman rose then with a smile and Fury shook hands with him across the desk. "Amber's been telling me all about you, Mr. Fury. You're certainly welcome in my house."

"Thank you."

Satchell waved Fury to sit down in a companion armchair. "Drink, Mr. Fury?" he asked, taking his seat again.

"Sherry, please," said Fury.

"Make it three, then, dear." Amber went to a sideboard. Satchell leaned forward. *"Were* you asked any embarrassing questions?"

"None that I couldn't handle."

Satchell leaned back and addressed Amber. "I don't like that man," he said. "Haskins. Attache to the Foreign Office here, Mr. Fury. I know he must be invited to these gatherings, but every time he comes he starts sucking up to me in a hand-and-foot manner I detest." He grinned ironically. "I'm glad they don't make them like *that* anymore."

"He's only trying to be helpful," said Amber from across the room. "I don't think he likes parties."

Satchell sighed. "Well," he said to Fury, "on to more important matters. First, my congratulations to you."

"For what?"

Satchell smiled at Amber as he took the drink from her. He paused, then said to Fury as Amber handed him a drink and sat down again, "You'll understand what for when I say that Mr. Middlemay would not have been *my* choice for the task he performed."

Fury glanced at Amber, who remained silent. "I see," he replied.

"I might also commend you on your patience and restraint in the matter of Mr. Middlemay."

Fury lit a cigarette. "Are you his superior?"

Satchell chuckled. "It's tempting to say in every which way." He sampled his drink. "No, not his direct superior," he continued. "I won't reveal my exact operational function, but I am a director of a Colony bureau which concerns itself with population and demographics. Amber is my best right hand. That is how we are known to most of my guests outside. Which particular population and the livelihood in which it is employed I will leave to you to infer. And before you perhaps conclude that I'm being lax about security, I'm being retired in two months' time. The opposition hardly ever bothers pensioned spies, least of all one who chooses to become a bi-weekly columnist for certain London newspapers." He paused for another tip of the glass.

"Second matter," he continued. "I invited you here this evening to personally caution you."

"Against reprisals?"

"Against reprisals," said Satchell. "From two possible directions. Of course, I can't compel you to sign an Official Secrets oath as you're not a British or Commonwealth subject. However, you *are* the crux of a somewhat sensitive incident. There really isn't any argument from our point of view that I can offer to convince you of the delicacy of the matter. But I must stress the fact that while your actual role has been officially diminished to the point of non-participation, you do remain in danger. From Peking, but most especially the Russians. They'd love to lay hands on an insider right now. They smell a lot of salt around the Bluelist-Felicity blow-up. I don't need to remind you of Soviet-Peking relations and how acid they are. They'd have had it out hammer and tongs long ago if they weren't both so interested in the West, wealthy fool that it is. It isn't an issue of us versus them any longer, Mr. Fury. It's a competition between Moscow and Peking over who is going to 'Win the West.'"

Satchell finished his drink, and shook his head at Amber's

silent query. "Now, here in Hong Kong the Russians are almost completely absent. Peking's influence is such that it has barred them from establishing an effective base of operations. Not even Soviet merchant vessels may call here. The Soviets have several bases of operations throughout the rest of Asia—most notably in Singapore—but in Hong Kong they're taboo. They'd do anything for just one scrap of information about Peking's or anyone else's activities here. So, if they ever learned of your role in the Felicity collapse and the Houghton-Devane scandal, you could be sure of being contacted by them someday. I wouldn't imagine it would be a very pleasant contact, either."

Fury considered an answer with a sip of his sherry. He said, "I don't mind not being mentioned in dispatches, just as long as the thing is done."

Satchell grunted agreement and approval. "To continue: You're safe from the Soviets and Peking, however—" He stopped when Fury frowned. "You have a question, Mr. Fury?"

"Two," replied Fury. "See Pok and Lon Ping: They didn't know me as well as Briscoe did—but Briscoe is talkative."

Satchell gave a brief chuckle. "Good point, Mr. Fury. But no worry. Mr. Ping has returned from whence he came. And See Pok is dead."

"Dead?"

"Yes," said Amber. "He owned a restaurant here called the Gorgon's Head. There was a fire there very early Friday morning. One body was found in the ashes—in the manager's office—and it was identified as See Pok's. He had been shot in the back."

"Briscoe?"

"We aren't sure," said Satchell. "Briscoe could have done it, or Peking may have ordered Pok's death. At this point in time it doesn't matter which is true. Pok's loss will not be much missed in the justice budgets. However, as I was saying, all the guilty parties in London have been removed from their posts or otherwise checkmated. But some of them may have had more advance warning of the collapse than others. We believe they issued final instructions to their field agents stationed here and throughout the Far East. Some of these people have assumed all along that the orders and tasks which they have undertaken for years from London were in the best interests of their country. Other agents are, more or less, co-conspirators. Who *these* people are and what are their final instructions we've yet to determine, and that task may take years."

Satchell finished his drink, then glanced at his watch. "That's about it for the moment, Mr. Fury," he said, rising. "Amber has something to tell you, and I myself would like to make your further acquaintance, but if we remain incommunicado any longer my guests will certainly begin to wonder. We'll talk later. It's going to be a long evening."

When the door closed behind Satchell, Fury set down his drink and cigarette and went to Amber to embrace her. After a long moment they both sighed, and he held her away from him by the shoulders. "I have something for you," he said, letting her go to reach into one of his pockets.

She laid a hand on his arm and deftly hooked her arm to his. "Not now, love. You heard Uncle John. We must go outside and make a show of enjoying ourselves."

"*I* won't need to act," he said as they approached the doors. "And you must promise me never to disappear again."

"I won't, Merritt. Not ever again. Not after tonight."

✻   ✻   ✻   ✻   ✻

They collected cocktails and went out to a corner of the veranda. The orchestra had retired its string section for the moment and the brass was blaring out an appealing, Latin-sounding dance number. Fury glanced once at the scene, then smiled at Amber as she leaned on the wall. "A very expensive ruse," he remarked.

"Oh, no," she said. "The party is genuine. Briscoe has been invited, too."

"I'd count on his very late arrival."

Amber shook her head. "He intends to crash it."

"Crash a party he's been invited to?"

"By blowing it up. He had explosives planted beneath this house."

Fury studied her for a moment. "Every party has its clown."

"Funny enough to destroy the foundations and send the rubble clattering down the slopes with all hands on board." She added, "I even ordered the explosives for him."

"What?"

"There's no danger now. The charges have been made harmless. No one but Uncle John knows about the explosives or how useless they are."

Fury let out a sigh of relief. "How did he expect to set them off?"

"With a remote pocket transmitter he's keeping with him. I suggested that, too. I was so convincing about wanting to destroy a Communist party! He said the Secret Service needs more people like me."

Fury shook his head. "But—*what for?*"

Amber smiled unconcernedly. "He thinks I have arranged for his escape through Macao tonight to the mainland. Before he goes, though, he wants to retrieve some personal papers he hid and some very valuable antiques from his house. He knew he could not come near here, so he had the explosives planted—Uncle John and his family were out yesterday and their servants had the day off. Then, through me, he warned the others that if he was interfered with in the least while he was in the house, he would blow the Satchells and their guests up. He said he would do it even if he *thought* they had been warned. He didn't let anyone know what he had planned until late this afternoon. Not even me."

"Does he know that your godfather is one of you?"

"Not in the least—not even that he is my godfather."

Fury lit another cigarette, then took a sip of his cocktail. "Is my being here part of his ruse or yours?"

"His." Amber chuckled. "He hates you, Merritt. He hates you so much that he wants to take you with him to the mainland."

"So he had you send that invitation to me."

"Yes. I would have had you invited anyway."

"How does he plan to kidnap me this time?"

Amber laughed. "I'm supposed to meet you and seduce you, Merritt. I must lure you over to his grounds sometime this evening to . . . indulge in an intense relationship. When you are too weak with worship to do anything but stand on your feet, I'm to draw a gun on you and march you into his house."

"Good God," exclaimed Fury. "Was that his idea?"

"No, that was mine, too. Almost everything I suggested he agreed to."

"I'll guarantee him an intense relationship, all right," chuckled Fury. He paused. "Why has he so much confidence in you, Amber? Hasn't he any idea of what we are to each other?"

"Not in the least."

"Have you seen him?"

She shook her head. "I have spoken with him over the telephone. If I had been able to see him, that would have been the end of him then and there."

"So I'm really to go over there with you?"

"If you choose. I would like you to be with me. It would serve Briscoe right to see the completeness of his folly."

"Just in time to see the police swoop down and apprehend him. Or is he to get the Carlton treatment?"

"Five minutes after Uncle sees us enter the house, he will signal the police to move in. We should have him under control by then."

Fury put his drink down on the wall and held her by the waist. Searching her open, placid face, he smiled. "Your superiors expect a lot from you."

"And they get it."

"Then what?"

"When it is finished, we return here to enjoy the party," she whispered. "Then I will take a much-deserved vacation and be a piece of your luggage. Do you think you would have much trouble passing me through Customs?"

"No, but if they expect me to pay a tax on you, they're crazy. Speaking of customs," said Fury, reaching into his jacket pocket again, "I have one here for you."

And that was when he gave her the diamond-studded gold band.

* * * * *

It was an interesting evening for Fury, and he surprised himself with how much he enjoyed it. The Satchells introduced him to a number of prominent persons, and Amber had refrained from mentioning the ring and its implications. He was grateful for that. She wore the ring but nobody seemed to notice it. She'd rather announce their impending marriage tomorrow, after the business with Briscoe was over.

But Annette Hitchings had the wonderful, admirable audacity to cut in on Amber during a dance, and Amber had the grace of confidence to defer. Annette leaned her head on his shoulder and said, as they moved, "You must think me terribly forward, Merritt."

"Terribly," he chuckled.

"I really don't carry on like this for every man I meet."

"I didn't think you did."

She raised her head and looked at him. "Thank you, dear. I was afraid you might have thought I was just a middle-aged flirt of no particular scruple."

"I'm very choosey with the women who throw themselves at me."

Miss Hitchings' eyes softened. "I know about you and Amber. She showed me the ring while you were being bored by poor Mr. Menzies a while ago. I won't tell anyone else. But I'll envy her for having the chance to know you the way I won't ever now." She paused. "Well, I was in your arms at least once, and you in mine. I'll treasure the memory."

Fury held her closer in genuine affection until the end of the number.

He went with Amber later to the buffet for their first snacks, then took them to one of the café tables on a part of the veranda that faced Briscoe's house. Fury glanced at his watch: eleven-thirty. He asked, as they sat down, "When do we rendezvous with Harry?"

"In another half hour," said Amber. "He's already here."

"Where are you packing it this time?"

"My gun? In my purse. I have one for you, too, Merritt, though it is not likely you will need it."

Fury considered his salad, then frowned. "Why is it necessary for us to go in at all? He's there. Why not just have the authorities surround the house and go in for him?"

Amber sampled the wine, and shook her head. "No, no, Merritt. He might hurt himself, he might try to kill himself. Personally, I would sooner see him shot, but what he knows is valuable to London. They want to know what he has done—everything over the years—and they want to study his organization so they can try to prevent it from ever happening again."

Fury looked over in the direction of Briscoe's house. There

was little he could see; tall trees and shrubbery on both grounds obscured what was already a black hulk against the brightly lit southeastern portion of the island below. "You said that he was coming to collect some antiques," he said. "How does he plan to take those north? Wouldn't he have enough of a problem just getting himself across?"

"He will have brought a van with a driver to take what he selects to somewhere in Kowloon to be crated. He told me that Ping gave him the diplomatic papers necessary to have the crate flown to Peking or shipped to Canton by rail." Amber sighed. "I have never dealt with a calmer man than Briscoe. He is simply not concerned with being apprehended; he thinks he has us under his thumb. I'll be so glad when it is over and finished."

Fury finished his snack and had another glass of wine with a cigarette, then sat back in his chair and relaxed, enjoying the warm air, the music, the sound of laughter and chatter, and the view, which necessarily included Amber.

He forgot time, Bluelist, Mr. Emrick, and his purpose here, until Amber, snuffing out her cigarette, said, "Now we must dance with Briscoe."

闖撞聚會

Chapter 14

Due
Process

Fury felt uncomfortable with the ease with which they approached Briscoe's house. With Amber on his arm, they left Sir John on the patio, walked past other guests up his driveway, then down the road and onto the flagstone walkway that led to the massive oak doors of the place. Amber took his hand and led him through the darkness across the lawn around the side of the house, and they came to the point where the grass began sloping downward to the patio and the first terrace. From there they could see the pick-up van and a single form leaning on the rear doors, smoking casually. Then they walked softly across the patio and turned to the French doors, Amber's automatic out, Fury's in his trouser pocket, his hand resting on it. "You seem to have an endless supply of these," he'd commented when she gave it to him and went over the plan one last time.

"They are made in Hong Kong, and are very cheap. Don't forget now, I must have you covered with mine when we walk in. We can disarm him with no trouble when we have him in a crossfire."

The French doors were open, as they had expected. A single

lamp in the living room cast ominous shadows on Briscoe's displayed armory. Down the hall, past the wide steps leading to the guests' and servants' quarters, a thin band of light came from the open door of Briscoe's study. Also coming from the study was low music. Fury, moving slowly ahead of Amber, searched his memory. It was ironic, he thought, that the man would choose to listen to Mozart *minuet marches* on what might be his last night in the West.

Briscoe's study was much the same as Satchell's, though with far fewer books and with the exception of the stereo record player, whose dual speakers were lodged on a high shelf among books on either side of the room. On the right side of Briscoe's modest oak desk was an antique floor clock, and on the left an Art Nouveau sideboard. Briscoe himself, dressed in a brown suede jacket and a turtleneck sweater—it was the first time Fury had seen him in anything other than formal wear or business suits—was at the desk, his hands thrust forward and palms flat on the blotter, and staring angrily at them as they walked in. He looked very commanding, thought Fury. Oddly, too commanding.

"Here he is, sir," said Amber as they moved across the rug to him. "He caused no problems."

Their strategy was simply to keep the man at ease and away from any guns or weapons with which he might hurt somebody or himself, until the police and Satchell's men came in five minutes. Fury could see his function clearly, now: He was the watch that was intended to hypnotize Briscoe. He hoped that his scowl of betrayal was credible. But something was wrong with Briscoe; his sight was fixed on neither Amber nor himself, but on the space between them.

Amber's face froze when a voice behind them addressed her in Chinese. Her eyes caught Briscoe's for the first time; he nodded twice. Fury understood then that it was not anger in his eyes, but fear. Amber dropped her gun, and turned around.

Fury turned with her. Stepping out of a dark corner was Lon Ping, dressed in spotlessly cleaned and pressed workman's clothes, holding an ugly machine pistol. He closed the study door first, then moved to the middle of the room and smiled congenially. "Please be seated," he said, motioning with the pistol to two armchairs in front of Briscoe's desk. "We have time. We await one last person, who will help me escort you all to the docks."

The situation had changed radically. Lon Ping, it had been assumed, had flown back to Peking, or at least had lost enough face to keep him out of circulation. He was present, though, thoroughly accounted for, armed, and curiously dressed. Odder still was the fact that Briscoe was under Ping's gun.

Ping smiled with fatherly tenderness at Amber. "My child," he said, "what fantastic story did my friend Harry tell you to bring you here with this inconvenient man?" He glanced at Fury.

Amber said nothing.

Ping said, "Miss Lee, I know you are a loyal, dedicated worker for the British Secret Service, and that my friend Harry is, too. He is your superior, and he gave you instructions."

"Leave her alone," said Briscoe.

Ping shrugged. "It matters not. I know what he told you. He was in grave danger of being killed by fanatical Communist agents, and he was going to the People's Republic to hide and wreck havoc. Is that what he told you?"

It was, thought Fury. Amber had moved away from her gun to an armchair on Briscoe's right. Fury, inwardly tense now, had moved to the other armchair but instead leaned back on Briscoe's desk, his hand still on the gun in his pocket, the safety off. He said, "Am I now *your* prisoner, Ping? I seem to have won some kind of popularity contest."

"That would seem to be apparent," replied Ping, bowing his head slightly. "My warmest congratulations, Mr. Fury—or whoever you really are."

Fury chuckled. "So, you really *can* talk."

"I am able to make the best conversation. We shall *all* be making conversation soon. Few of those present, however, will live to converse to anyone's enlightenment."

Fury chuckled again. "No, I suppose not. I don't imagine you people stock many Mao tunics in my or Mr. Briscoe's sizes. So if the clothes don't fit, adjust the population instead of the stock. A highly original inventory philosophy."

At that moment Briscoe exploded behind him, venting the pent-up anger that had hid behind the fear. "Boy, have you got it wrong, Fury! Totally wrong! This tricksy son of a bitch is taking us to *Moscow*, Fury—*Moscow!!* He and that driver he sent me and a few of his buddies on the Kowloon docks! This two-timing bastard had it all planned! Who do I find waiting for me when I walk in here an hour ago?? *Him*, that's who! And what does he tell me? That he's defecting to the Russians, and that he's taking me and you and Miss Lee with him—as peace offerings! Pok's dead, you know, he's dead as hell, and guess who killed him?? Old Ping, here, the son of a bitch killed his own goddamned man—but not before he had him arrange cabins for us on one of Pok's own freighters, which so conveniently leaves tonight, calls on Singapore, where we so gaily transfer to some goddamned Russian freighter heading home for Vladivostok!!"

Ping smiled. "I seem to recall something the wise but unfortunate Mr. Fury said to you the other day, Harry. Something about fools and dupes. Please, do not bore us with your outrage. You duped Mr. Fury, but worst of all, in my modest eyes at least, you duped Miss Lee and your own country."

Briscoe suddenly rose from the desk and shot a fist at Ping. "Too afraid to go back to the bloody People's Paradise, Ping?? I know why, too! You'd be sent to Coventry for this mess, wouldn't you?? Or maybe to your goddamned grave! You pious-faced son of a bitch, you—"

Ping frowned mockingly. "Traitor, *Sir* Harry?" he interjected. "Turncoat? Judas? Knave? Blackguard?" He shook his head in appreciation. "How wonderful is the English vocabulary! So many synonyms in it that may also be applied to yourself!"

Briscoe slapped the top of the desk with his open hands. "I *trusted* you, Ping! It wasn't even an issue of trust! I was willing to *help* you people catch up with the world! To the bloody limit!"

Ping shrugged. "Circumstances have changed, Harry. As well you know. Our common and incomparable acquaintance, Mr. Fury here, has seen to that. I think my friends in Moscow will find him very interesting. I believe, Harry, that Lenin had many things to say on the subjects of trust and deceit, but I am not a Party scholar and so not able to offer his wisdom in rebuttal."

Briscoe leaned over the desk again and shook his fist. "You smug son of—"

Ping's eyes narrowed then. "Be quiet," he said calmly, then fired a single shot in Briscoe's direction and once at the stereo turn-table. The first slug struck some panelling above Briscoe's head, warping the wood and showering splinters over Briscoe and his desk. Briscoe, his eyes wide, slowly sank back into his chair. The second slug smashed the tone arm of the stereo, ending the music with a squeal.

The shots caused Fury to make a decision. What Ping's slug had done to the thick panelling was to reveal that the bullets were dum-dums, slugs which exploded on contact inside whatever they hit. They could do worse than disfigure a body. One was enough, but Ping's was a machine pistol.

It was this second fact that affected his decision more than the first. Ping's machine pistol was on semi-automatic. It was a stupid thing to have done, under the circumstances. Ping must have chosen the weapon to better cover all the "guests" he was expecting, but had forgotten to put it on automatic. It was always careless to forget the purpose of one's choice of weapons. And there was no one else here to cause Ping to regret his negligence.

So Fury, casually moving a step away from the desk to the armchair, asked, almost contemptuously, "Shouldn't that thing be on automatic, Mr. Ping?"

It worked. Mildly startled first by Fury's question, then by its import, Ping's glance darted down to the side of the pistol while his other hand reached up to flick the lever up one more notch.

It was enough time. Ping sensed then what was about to happen but hesitated between firing and notching up the lever. Fury fell to his haunches as he brought the pitiful little black automatic from his pocket and fired rapidly at Ping, emptying the clip. There was no time and less chance to do anything fancier than just fire at Ping. At first he didn't think the slugs had even penetrated Ping's denim jacket because the little gun hardly bucked in his grip.

But Ping fell to the rug.

Fury jumped up and bolted for the machine pistol that lay useless in the man's hand. Snatching it away, he saw that he had put an irregular circle of holes in Ping's chest, and that the man was still breathing. Ping looked back up at Fury with a strange kind of conviction in his eyes. He rasped with bitter, knowing finality, "I knew you meant death the first I saw you."

Then Ping's eyes glazed over. Something bulging in his breast pocket caught Fury's eye. He reached down and took it out. It was an extra clip for the pistol and something that looked like a portable tape secretary, except that it had a retractable antenna. The front of it had been smashed by one of his slugs, just below a blue button that was covered by a plastic flip-up guard. He realized then what it was: Briscoe's detonator.

"Merritt!!" screamed Amber. "Look out!!"

Another explosion galvanized all his senses. He jumped up with the device in one hand and the machine pistol in the other.

The .45 in Briscoe's grip must have been in one of the desk drawers, and part of his anger must have stemmed from his not being able to touch it under Ping's scrutiny. He was still behind the desk, smiling slyly at Fury, waiting.

Amber lay on the rug between them, on her back. Beneath it Fury could see the red stain spreading fast. She'd retrieved her gun—he remembered her diving for it the second he had rushed Ping—but had paused too long to watch him bent over him. The force of the impact of Briscoe's slug had spun her completely around and her little automatic had flown from her hand and bounced onto the rug near the sideboard. She was still breathing.

Fury stood stock still. Briscoe said, "Took me a while to catch on, my friend—" he was back to normal now—"but I doubt if she could have adequately explained to me what *you* were doing with a gun when she was to have made damned certain in her most professional way that *you* were in no condition to be doing *any* fast thinking. It all makes sense now, my friend! Every bit of it! *She* killed Carlton, didn't she? *She* put you up that night, didn't she?? The two-timing bitch!" Briscoe laughed triumphantly. "Don't look so cross with me, Merritt! It was your quick-draw on old Ping that made me see the light. You saved my life, you know. Can't fault me for putting two and two together." He stopped then, and frowned. "Thanks for the heroism, but now kindly drop that gun and hand over that radio thing. Gently."

Fury cocked his head. "Why don't you shoot, Harry?"

"Because I want you to observe something first."

Fury shook his head. "My option." He flicked up the

plastic guard with his thumb.

"Don't!!" cried Briscoe, his features slackening.

Fury pressed the button. Briscoe flinched.

But there was no faraway concussion. Briscoe blinked in wonder.

And as he blinked, Fury pulled the trigger of the pistol and fired at Briscoe's hand. The heavy gun clattered to the desk and Briscoe clutched at his injured wrist.

Fury dropped the device, approached the desk wordlessly, and pitched the .45 across the room to a corner. Just then they heard gunfire from outside the house. Fury backed away, the pistol still covering Briscoe, and stooped down beside Amber. Before he could touch her wrist, he saw that she had stopped breathing. The diamonds on the gold band on her finger sparkled dully in the dim light.

Briscoe, not moving, heard Fury sigh, and watched closely how one side of his face pulsed in what he knew was pain. As Fury stood up again, he noticed, too, that the gunfire outside had ceased and had been replaced by voices giving orders from inside the house. The look in Fury's eyes was far away but too close to Briscoe's intelligence. He knew the look. He'd seen it that first afternoon in the board room. He regretted not having taken it seriously then. So much trouble could have been avoided.

Fury took another step back, reaching up with his other hand to click the lever on the pistol up one last notch.

"*In here!!*" bellowed Briscoe. He was sweating now. "*In the study!! For God's sake, hurry!!*" Meekly, half-humorously, he said to Fury, "I—I have a right to a trial, old man. To due process, you know. I *really do.*"

Fury's brow knotted even more tightly. "Don't be facetious, Harry." Then, with both hands gripping the pistol, he took careful aim and squeezed the trigger.

正規

Epilogue

We Remain

One Sunday evening in January, driven by a restless curiosity and a plain desire to be outside, Merritt Fury left his suite in the Mandarin and went strolling through the deserted bazaars near the Central District. A heavy downpour had drenched the city for nearly twenty-four hours without letup and stopped only an hour ago. It was warm and cloudless now, and the wet sidewalks glistened with neon light. Most shops were closed and virtually the only other people in the streets were random tourists. He walked leisurely, stopping now and then to peer through the windows at the candy displays of the vacant counters, grunting satisfaction whenever he spied the bright blue wrappers of Blue Lake Chocolate Bars.

In time he came upon the burnt-out shell of the Gorgon's Head. The bronze doors had been replaced with plywood, and the tiny porthole windows high off the pavement were blank, drafty holes where birds had built nests. The grotesque Gorgon's head was gone; the alcove where it used to sit was dark and strewn with rubbish. But the building seemed structurally intact. With some work, he thought, it could be converted into a movie house.

He lit a cigarette, and the flare of his lighter reflected from a pair of yellow eyes that stared unblinkingly at him from low in the alcove. Then a sleek black cat jumped out of the darkness onto the empty pedestal, where it sat on its haunches and closed its eyes once in that languid, contented way he'd always found attractive in cats. He stooped down and extended a hand to pet it. It nuzzled the open palm of his hand in gratitude, and purred so hungrily that its whole body seemed to vibrate.

He scratched the fur on the animal's head, and smiled wistfully up at the searchlights sweeping the sky above him.

He wondered where the guns were whispering now.

THE END

仍留如故